when
love
calls, you
better
answer

also by bertice berry

Jim and Louella's Homemade Heart-fix Remedy

The Haunting of Hip Hop

Redemption Song

You Still Ghetto: You Know You're Ghetto If. . .

I'm On My Way but Your Foot Is on My Head: A Black Woman's Story of Getting Over Life's Hurdles

Sckraight from the Ghetto: You Know You're Ghetto If . . .

Bertice: The World According to Me

A NOVEL

when love calls, you better answer

BERTICE BERRY

BROADWAY BOOKS NEW YORK

BROADWAY

WHEN LOVE CALLS, YOU BETTER ANSWER. Copyright © 2005 by
Bertice Berry. All rights reserved. No part of this book may be reproduced or
transmitted in any form or by any means, electronic or mechanical, including
photocopying, recording, or by any information storage and retrieval system,
without written permission from the publisher. For information, address
Broadway Books, a division of Random House, Inc.

This book is a work of fiction. Names, characters, businesses, organizations,
places, events, and incidents either are the product of the author's imagination
or are used fictitiously. Any resemblance to actual persons, living or dead,
events, or locales is entirely coincidental.

PRINTED IN THE UNITED STATES OF AMERICA

Broadway Books and its logo, a letter B bisected on the diagonal, are
trademarks of Random House, Inc.

Visit our Web site at www.broadwaybooks.com

First edition published June 2005

Book design by Kathryn Parise

LIBRARY OF CONGRESS CATALOGING-IN-PUBLICATION DATA
Berry, Bertice.
    When love calls you better answer : a novel / Bertice Berry.— 1st ed.
        p.   cm.
    ISBN 0-385-51083-7
    1.   African American women—Fiction. I. Title.
PS3552.E7425W47 2005
813'.54—dc22

                                                                    2004058639

10 9 8 7 6 5 4 3 2

For Beatrice Berry, Jeanine Chambers, Ptosha (Rocki) Rockingham,
William, Mariah, Jabril and Fatima, the world's greatest movers.
And to Terry Evenson and the ancestors who move my spirit.

Real love, true love don't call on everybody, 'cause everybody ain't always ready. But when it do call, when it says your name, you better answer.

—AUNT BABE

go back to get forward

When a painful story is told out loud, it sets some-body free. Sometimes it's the storyteller, most times though, it's the listener. They say that if we honor the ancestors with our lives, then will they honor us with their stories.

—AUNT BABE

My name is Shoulda Been Wright. I married a Wright, but my daddy said that I should have been a boy, so he named me Shoulda Been. I'm dead. Been that way for some time now, but dead ain't never mean done—it just puts you closer to truth, closer to life.

The story I'm telling is not about me, but then again it is. My niece, Bernita, is the flip side of my coin. I had a lot of men because I was afraid that nobody would ever really love me. She had a lot 'cause she was afraid to really love. Bernita is the reason I'm here, 'cause what don't get done in this life is passed down to the next generation. If you ain't had no children of your own, then it's passed down to your family's children.

Bernita is my sister Buster's child. Now, don't get to thinking that I'm from a crazy family 'cause we got a bunch of funny names. What you name a child is important, but how you treat them is bigger. Having a different-sounding name ain't what makes you bad. Just think about people like Condoleezza, Oprah, and Colin. Them names ain't no different. We just don't have a problem saying difficult names if they attached to money and power. But now you take them young Shaniquas and Tyreeses—hey, I wonder if the plural of Tyreese is Tyerye—anyway, those kids get pulled into thinking that they are less than a Bob or Mary, and then they start to acting like they are. That's what they call a self-fulfilling prophecy. Whew, now that's a big one. Hearing me talk, you probably thinking I'm a ball of contradictions. But if you're really listening, then you know that wisdom don't just come from college classrooms.

Even though I didn't like school I always liked reading and learning, and I can still bust a verb with the best of them. It's good to be book smart, but it's even better to combine that with spirit and life. Anyway, my sister Buster had one child, and one child only. She had that child just to prove to my sister Ronnie that she could.

Bernita was born fussing. She cried day and night. The only thing that seemed to quiet her down was that baby buggy. Whenever I would walk with her, she got to cooing and smiling, like she was pure joy and light. I guess every child is. But I was just a kid myself, and when my sister Buster was working and come to think of it, even when she wasn't, I was the one who watched Bernita. I didn't like Bernita from day one. Mind you, I didn't hate her; I just didn't like her.

Before you get to thinking that I felt like that 'cause Bernita stole my place as the baby in the family, think on this—when you living in a house that's headed up by hate, ain't nobody the apple of anybody's eye. We were all too busy trying to judge my daddy's moods. My daddy—would say "rest his soul," but I know for a fact that his soul ain't resting—was mean as they came. He could be peaceful one minute and then he'd up and smack you for no cause at all. Maybe he had a reason, but we never knew what it was.

I was the last of eight girls. We lived in Sylvania, Georgia, in a house that was too big to be small and too small to be big. It was somewhere in the middle. That was the only thing that was average about us. Everything else was high drama. It wasn't the everyday soap opera kind. No sir, no ma'am. We had that *Sunset Boulevard* drama. Wasn't nothing normal. Sometimes he would come home cussing and fussing. Other times, he would drag in all slow, get a plate of food, and go to his room. I preferred the cussing. If he was dragging, it just meant that the storm was coming later. And storms that come in the night always seem bigger and blacker than if they come in the day.

By the time Bernita was born my daddy had settled down some. But that's like saying Hitler was nicer in his later years. Anyway, it was my job to try to keep Bernita quiet so she wouldn't set my daddy off. Since almost anything could set him off, I knew the best thing to do when he was there was to leave. I would take Bernita to the park in that buggy of hers where everybody would say how cute she was. Of course, that made me like her even less. But it was in the park that I found out that Bernita was good for something. Sometimes, grown men would come up and say how pretty she was. Sometimes, they would ask if she was mine. The first time someone asked, I told the man he must be crazy. I call him a man 'cause he looked past twenty, but not old enough to really be grown.

"I'm just a kid myself, mister," I said.

He looked at me real hard and got to grinning like he knew something I didn't. "Well," he said, still smiling with teeth that were too big for his own mouth, "sometimes, young girls like doing *it*."

Now back then, I didn't really know what "it" was. I'd heard my sisters talking about this "it," and I think I heard my mama and daddy doing "it." My sisters made this thing sound like you had to be a part of a secret organization that only older girls could get into before you could know what it was. There was something in the way they talked about "it" that made me think of something special, like mashed sweet potatoes on a Tuesday night. (We only had them on Sundays and Thanksgiving.) Some foods are all in the taste, but some are in how they feel too. Mashed sweets are like that. I would close my eyes and let that top layer of crispy buttery crust snap in my mouth, so the soft sweetness would melt through. Getting something like that on a regular Tuesday sure would have been nice.

The man in the park with the big teeth was smiling harder 'cause when he said that about young girls liking to do "it," I was thinking 'bout them mashed sweets, but he thought that I was thinking bout "it." I had one hand on Bernita's buggy and the other one on my hip when I heard him say, "You cute too."

He was the first man to show me any attention, and as it turned out, the first one I did "it" with. I was thirteen and Bernita wasn't no more than a year old. It sure changed me, and I know now that it changed her too. 'Cause when he took me to the park bathroom, Bernita was right there with me. She may have just been a baby, but believe me when I tell you, babies see what's going on.

Now if you asked most folks, they would say that man raped

me. Considering the difference in our age and the wisdom he was supposed to have, I guess he did. But I'm gonna tell the truth, 'cause that's all I can tell you. I liked what he did. Not the physical part, 'cause that hurt me real hard. I liked that this man was being nice to me, and saying sweet things.

If a girl don't hear the kindness she needs to hear from the right man, she will look to hear it from any man.

The time I was with him wasn't that long. But he kept telling me that I was pretty and that he was going to do things for me, 'cause I deserved them. But after that, I never saw him again. I went to the park time and again hoping to find him, but he didn't come back. After a while I figured he must have found somebody that he liked better than me.

I never even knew his name.

Well, I said that I was gonna tell you about my niece Bernita, and I am. But you can't understand her life 'til you understand mine and see where hers came from. Bernita's mama, Buster, didn't like her daughter all that much neither. My sister was too much like her name, a regular buster. One day she started going to see a woman everybody said was funny. There wasn't nothing 'bout her that made me laugh though. That woman was tough like my daddy, but she was real sweet on Bernita. Which made her nothing like my daddy when I think of it, 'cause he wasn't sweet on nobody. Whenever my daddy was in one of his ways, Buster would go over to Miss Eudora's house.

"I'm outta here," she would say, walking just like my daddy. "I don't need to hear none of this mess. I work hard too. Babe, you take care of Bernie and make sure that she gets something to eat."

I wanted to tell her to feed her own child. But then I would remember the nameless man with the big grin and pretty words. I figured that it was Bernita that brought him to me the first time and maybe she could do it again.

Well, like I said, that man never did come back, but I met others. They all said the same stuff. But with them, I made sure I got a name first. I knew that most times it wasn't their real name, but at least I had a word to go with my thoughts. Later on I would imagine that I was Mrs. Jim Wilson, or Mrs. Clarence White. None of them men would've ever married me. I know that now, but I was just trying to have something to believe in.

In my mind, they were all the first man with the big grin. By the time I realized that they didn't care nothing about me, and that they were just getting what they wanted, I had nicknames, and a reputation to match. I was "Miss Hot Pants" or "Miss Too Hot to Trot." The girls were more creative than the boys and meaner too. They called me "Peanut Butter," because they said I spread easy.

Now, you may be wondering where my mother and sisters were when all of this was going on. You probably thinking that somebody in my house should have known something. Well, someone did, but by then, she was just five years old.

generational pain

Ain't no hurt like an old hurt.

—BEATRICE BERRY

Folks say that childbirth is natural. I say it's a miracle. Ain't nothing natural *or* normal about what happens to women when they give birth. Now, I bet you wondering how I know about it since I ain't had no children of my own. That's something I need to tell you 'bout. You see, over here on the other side, we can see some of everything. We can call up a memory and see it from start to finish. Even if I wasn't dead when it happened. I can even get a hold of the thoughts of the folks I'm connected to. That sure is something. That's why it ain't right for the living to do too much meddling with the dead. It upsets the balance of life. If you could see and know all that we do from the other side, there really wouldn't be a reason to keep on living. Nor would you want to. There's no sorrow over here. But just because you shouldn't meddle too much doesn't mean we can't. No sir, more you learn about your ancestors, more you learn about yourself.

That's how I got to help my Bernita, but I'm a bit ahead of myself. I was telling you about my mama. After the birth of all her girls, my mama, rest her soul (I know for a *fact* she is resting real good. And she's in charge of the Bingo hall over here to boot), would go through what the old folks called "dark patches." After she had me, my daddy told her that I was gonna be just like her, good for nothing. From then on, her dark patches were more like the whole cloth. If I didn't know better, I would say that what my daddy prophesized had come true. But I know better, so I can tell you the truth; that he knew what was 'bout to happen because he made it happen. It's like somebody yelling, "Look out, you're gonna fall," then pushing you down. He did the same thing to me, but while his bitterness killed my mama, that same bitterness is what I used to live.

My daddy used to yell at my mama something fierce. To hear him tell it, she never moved fast enough, or did anything right. To make *his* matters worse (according to him), she went and brought him a bunch of girls when all my daddy wanted was a boy. Just one would have been enough. Well, one day my mama got the strength to tell him how low he was. She said that the only thing she done wrong was to marry him. And she only married him 'cause nobody else had asked her, and she was afraid that nobody else ever would. I'm sure you know people like that. I'm a tell you something that I learned late in life—don't settle for the "it'll do." That's what I call something that you just put up with, on account of you ain't got what you really need. You can't make somebody wrong for you into somebody right, and my mama found that out firsthand. She told my daddy all that and a bunch of other stuff too. She got herself real worked up. Just when my daddy was about to put a stop to all her sassing, God up and took her home. I guess she was kind of praying for that.

The doctor said that she died from a heart attack, but I know it wasn't nothing of the kind. Attacks come quick and take you by surprise. What killed my mama had been happening for some time.

You would think that my mama dying the way that she did would have done something to make my daddy change. Well, he did, but it sure wasn't for the better. My daddy kept his meanness, but then he started getting the same dark patches my mama had. He got worse and my sisters got gone until it was just me, Buster, and Bernita left, but Buster wasn't around that much. So it was really just me and the baby.

Bernita grew up in a house of pain. Her granddaddy was mean and mad. Her mother, my sister Buster, was usually nowhere to be found. And me, I was the town whore. Bernita was seeing me go from one bed to the next. At the time, I thought I was doing what I wanted to do and that all that bed hopping made me free. But all it did was give me more pain. With each man came another promise of lasting love, and for that moment, I lied to myself and tried to believe that maybe this one will stay. But it was always the same. People got to saying that Bernita was mine. They figured I was fast enough to have had plenty babies. But that was one thing I never went through. I know it was nobody but God that kept it from happening. The men who came around didn't like using no protection. They said that they wanted to feel all of my sweetness around them.

Wasn't nothing sweet about it, 'cause they pleasure was my sadness.

crabs in a barrel

*If you can't fly, don't go shooting nobody else
down from the sky.*

—AUNT BABE

Bernita Brown, my niece, is a good example of how bad men can
happen to good women. Bernita is good through and through. All
she ever wanted to do was to make other folks happy. But in doing that, she forgot about herself. Sometimes I wonder how a child
who grew up in so much pain can try to see nothing but good.

Bernita always liked to read and she loved school more than any
of my sisters or their kids. She would go to bed without having to
be told. She got up the same way. When she was tall enough to
reach the washing machine and ironing board, Bernita was doing
laundry for everybody. She didn't ever have to be told to do her
chores. She did them because she wanted to and she wanted to escape her family. I came to understand that what other people took
as work, Bernita took as pleasure. The harder the task, the more joy
she got from it. I know now what I didn't know when I was alive.

It's like that with everything though. That's why there's no sorrow or pain over here. I learned that most sorrow comes from the pain that others pass on to you. And that pain comes from not knowing or understanding the cycle of pain. When I was walking among the living, all I knew was that I was hurting. I didn't see that the folks causing the pain were hurting too.

Bernita was as good at her schoolwork as she was at everything else. So much so that even though she didn't come from a family with much education, somebody saw fit to make sure that she got to go to college. She had a teacher by the name of Lee Morris. Mr. Morris took a liking to Bernita and it wasn't the kind that I had come accustomed to. He saw something in her besides a good girl with good grades. Mr. Morris saw through what she did and got a glimpse of how she felt. He saw her sadness.

Bernita had Mr. Morris for two classes. He taught English and science at the high school. Most teachers did double duty but Mr. Morris was also the principal. It was a poor school, but they gave the best that they could give. Well, Mr. Morris did his job. He taught Bernita and he watched as she turned the lessons into something else. She was never at the top of her class but she was smart enough that somebody should've took notice. Mr. Morris was the only one who did though. Bernita wasn't popular, and she didn't come from one of those important families, the kind that's slightly above everybody else. She was cute, but so is every other girl before they get beat down by life. Bernita didn't have any special talents that caused her to be noticed. She was just good. It's sure nice that she had Mr. Morris her last two years of high school. Otherwise, she probably would have ended up working in our hometown doing laundry for one of the hotels or something like that.

I remember the day Mr. Morris came to the house and asked my sister Buster why she wasn't helping Bernita with her college applications. He may as well have said, "Why haven't you been to the moon?" In Buster's mind, the moon and college were just as far away and just as hard to get to.

When Mr. Morris looked around our house, he could see the kind of spotlessness that comes from trying to make up for something that's missing. But underneath he could feel the hate and shame. The whole while Mr. Morris was talking about college, me and Buster was just sitting and staring. He must have seen that he wasn't getting through. He started to tell my sister not to worry about anything, because he would help Bernita with her applications, but right when he did, my daddy came rushing out of his room and the storm came rushing with him.

"I don't need some damned pervert all up in my business," he yelled. By then my daddy had gotten real old, but age didn't do nothing for his personality. Whenever I hear somebody say that folks mellow with age, I know that they don't understand that age ain't got nothing to do with it. Only love and wisdom can mellow hatred. My daddy didn't get no love, 'cause he never gave none.

Mr. Morris was looking for Buster to say something back to my daddy, but she didn't. She grabbed her jacket and said what she always did, "I'm outta here."

Mr. Morris picked up the college books that he'd brought and went on his way. He never said another word. Thank God actions speak louder.

Bernita had been listening from the bedroom she shared with me and her mother. She was seventeen years old, still sleeping on a pallet on the floor. Buster and I were grown women and we were still in beds that should have been passed down to Bernita. Even after all my other sisters had gone, we weren't allowed to move to another room.

"Why granddaddy always gotta be so mean?" Bernita asked. She wasn't really looking for no answer and back then, I wouldn't have had none to give her. I gave her a look that said, "You know how he is." Then I tried to make myself look busy. The simple truth was that even though this child had been a burden to me, she was still a child. And she had to endure my father's anger, and everyone else's bitterness. She didn't cuss, or yell back, none of the things I would have done at her age. She just went back to reading.

Now you would think that Mr. Morris's experience at my house would have made him look for a more appreciative family to help. No sir, no ma'am. Instead, he was more determined than before. Mr. Morris went above and beyond, and did what needed to be done. He called a college where a friend of his worked and told him all about Bernita. He filled out the application himself and paid for it. When Bernita got accepted, we did exactly what folks in a house full of hate would do: We laughed and made fun of her.

"How you going to college?" Buster asked. "I ain't paying for you to go off and come back actin' like you better than me."

"What she need more schoolin' for?" I said, "She already got a good job at the hotel. She can get full-time easy. She'll probably get supervisor before she twenty-five."

My father added his own brand of bitterness to what should have been Bernita's joy.

"Hell," he barked, "she ain't gonna do nothing but get pregnant like her mother did. I ain't raising no more of you nasty heifers."

Bernita didn't say a mumbling word. She gathered up the laundry, like she always did, and went to the basement to wash. I never did like that basement; it was dark and damp smelling. There was a working toilet in the corner that backed up whenever my father used it. The only light down there was the bulb that swung by a cord from the underside of the upstairs floorboards. That basement felt like the pit of my father's stomach and it smelled like it too. Somehow, Bernita turned that dark smelly basement into a place of refuge. She went there when the house was cold, or whenever I snuck a man in under my daddy's roof. It's something, now when I think about it. My father never called our house what it was or what it could have been. The word *home* never came from his mean lips. It was always "his roof." For Buster it was 635 C Street. I called it *there* like I'm going back *there*, or I can't wait to get out of there. It was never called *home*, because it never felt like one. Somehow though, Bernita made that basement special. She went there to think on her life and how she could make it better.

The night that we talked down her college dreams, she came up from that basement with a plan. She didn't look no different than she did when she went down there. She didn't say nothing to show that she agreed or disagreed with us. But the next morning just before she was gonna leave for school, she gave us all a piece of her mind.

"I'm glad that you all are so concerned for my future," she said with one hand on her hip. "But I can see by your lives that you don't have a future.

"Mama," she said, looking at Buster like she just figured out that they were related, "I don't need you to pay for anything. Mr. Morris got it all taken care of."

I gave her a sneaky look and said, "I bet I know how you got him to do that."

"No, Aunt Babe." Bernita was standing up to us for the first time in her short little life. "I don't do what you do to men to get them to like me. Besides, it doesn't even work for you."

Just then Buster slapped Bernita hard enough to make her fall, but Bernita just laughed real scary like.

Something inside me just snapped. I had exposed her to enough filth to hurt her in ways that couldn't be seen. I knew that then like I know it now. But at the time I chose to think about it another way.

"Well, you dirty bitch," I said. "After all I've done for you. I took care of your stinking ass when your own mama didn't want to have nothing to do with you."

I grabbed Bernita by the neck and tried to give her all the hurt that life had given me. I was mad because I had a Tom, a Dick, and a Harry but I didn't have a Mr. Morris. There was no one to help me get out of that bedroom. Deep inside I knew that Bernita was a good girl, and that made me even madder. I had allowed men to do all kinds of things to me but none of them had done anything *for* me. All Bernita had done was be herself and somebody saw that that was enough. Mr. Morris was just being hisself and doing his job when he decided to help Bernita and I had to see it as something dirty. Otherwise, I would have to face the truth about me, and the low and hollow life I had been living.

All of this was going through my head when I heard Buster yelling, "Stop, you gonna kill her." She pulled me off of Bernita and when I came to myself, I saw the damage I'd done. Bernita was bleeding from the back of her head where I had banged it on the floor. She was reaching out like she was trying to grab the air that I was keeping from her. There were bruises on her neck and face and scratches on her arms. Buster grabbed me and I saw blood on her hands and under her nails which told me that she had been responsible for Bernita's scratches too. On the day that should have been one of her best, Bernita's mother and aunt had beaten her because she wanted a better life. If it hadn't been for the fact that many black children were beaten the same way their parents had learned from slave masters long ago, maybe someone would have reported us. Then maybe somebody who knew better or wanted to would have been able to help. But no one did.

When you have a bad environment your whole childhood, even when you leave it, it don't always leave you.

CHAPTER 4

coming out of the dark

My soul looks back and wonders, how I got over.

—NEGRO SPIRITUAL

With the exception of stopping by to pick up her belongings, Bernita left our house without looking back. She stayed with Mr. Morris and his wife until it was time to leave for college. Mrs. Morris was as kind as her husband, and during those few short months, she showed Bernita the love that's supposed to come from a mother.

Mrs. Morris understood Bernita's pain because she had come up hard herself. When Bernita first got to the Morrises' house she was as cautious as she had been at the house where she grew up. That girl had been walking on eggshells from the time she first learned to toddle. Afraid that I might have been right about Mr. Morris, Bernita was barely able to look him in the eye. She would shower real fast, get dressed, and then would run across the hall to the sewing room that they'd turned into a room for her. Bernita would lock the door and pray that nobody would bother her.

One night after she came in from work, Bernita went into the Morrises's laundry room and commenced to washing clothes. Mrs. Morris came in and told her she didn't need to. Bernita explained that she had been doing laundry since she was knee high to a roach, though she didn't say it quite that way. "No matter," Mrs. Morris told her, "you go to school, you work, then you come home and clean. It's okay to rest, child."

Bernita surprised her own self when the tears began to pour down her cheeks like a sudden overflow of river water. It must have looked just like that to Mrs. Morris because Bernita had been calm right before the dam broke.

"Why y'all so nice to me?" she asked.

"Because you deserve it. And because I know you," Mrs. Morris said. She didn't tell Bernita all of her business, but I know just what happened. That's another good thing about learning a story when you're dead. You get insight that earthly beings miss. That song by Sweet Honey says to pay more attention to things than you do to beings. Sometimes when you listen to the rustle of the leaves, you can hear the dead talking.

Mrs. Morris grew up as Anna Louise Mason, and was an only child. Believe me when I tell you that was a blessing. Wasn't no need for more children to have to go through what she did. Now, just cause I know all of what happened, don't mean I need to give you every detail. Suffice it to say that that girl grew up in a middle-class home with a mother and father. She had everything a little black girl could have ever known to ask for. But she also got more than anybody would have ever wanted.

Most folks are used to hearing about daddies doing dirt. But Anna Louise's mother was the one who rolled in filth. She used that girl in ways that she shouldn't have, and then on Sundays her mama showed up in church like she was the one without sin.

Anna Louise Mason's mama thought she was upstanding and decent on account of she married the only black doctor in a black town. But God knows that woman had no reason to think herself decent. Mrs. Mason was what they call high yellow. She was real light skinned at a time when folks thought that meant something. Mr. Mason was blue black, and thought that by marrying his wife, he might somehow seem lighter. They didn't really like each other, but they both lived the lies they told themselves. You see, they thought that marriage to each other made them better. Don't get me wrong on this. I don't mean like when people get married and it helps to pull up the other person's strengths. I mean that Mrs. Mason thought that even though her husband was what her mother called "too black to see at night," his being a doctor made him not so dark and Mrs. Mason even more beautiful. On the other foot, Mr. Mason thought that even though Mrs. Mason wasn't smart or friendly, that her being high yellow made him less dark, and her more kind.

From where I'm sitting, I can see the danger that all this color thinking does to people who have already been hurt by they history. To be true to the story though, I gotta tell you that they both got their thinking honest. They learned and lived what they people's people had passed down to them.

Anna Louise wasn't born as light as her mama had hoped. So her mother took to bleaching her skin with everything from Clorox to what she called a "mild" mixture of milk, lye, and peroxide. When she wasn't bleaching Anna Louise, she was touching her in places and ways that shouldn't been touched for years to come. And surely not by her mama.

Anna Louise had bad skin and even worse feelings about herself.

What she did have going for her, though, was a real sharp mind. She used that mind to get out of her little town and away from her mother. She supported herself through college. Her father would send money from time to time, but he had to keep it from his wife. After Anna Louise left home her mother said, "If that black whore wants to run off on her own, let her take care of her own self."

Anna Louise worked hard and became a teacher, and that's how she met Mr. Morris. He looked past her blotchy skin and watery eyes and saw a heart that needed love. He asked her to marry him a week after they met. Anna Louise said yes and they got married seven days later. When they took Bernita in, they had already been married for twenty-seven years. They never had children though; something Anna Louise's mother did to her caused that to never be. Anna Louise didn't tell Bernita none of that, but I'm telling you so you can see how lives connect.

Anna Louise told Bernita that she grew up hard, but that Mr. Morris grew up in love and when he told Anna Louise about Bernita, something he said reminded Anna Louise of herself. "You have to help that girl," she told him. She was feeling the push from one of the ancestors over on the other side.

Anna Louise only took care of Bernita for a few months, but they stayed in touch right up until the day before she died. On that morning, Anna Louise called Bernita to tell her how she'd always be looking out for her, and the very next day she died. But I know for a fact that she kept her word. Anna Louise sure is something. She's a good friend of mine over here on the other side, and she's *still* looking out for Bernita.

Bernita went on to college in a small town in Missouri. The school was an all-women's school called Cotty College. It was as white as you please, but Bernita didn't have no problem adjusting to the color differences. She was too happy sleeping in a bed that was her own. That school was real good to Bernita. Besides all the good learning, the girls were like sisters to each other. Now, you may be thinking that she'd a been better off with black people. I'm a tell you this, she grew up with black folks, and she was a hell of a lot better off at that school. Don't get me wrong, ain't nothing like being around bright black folks. They bring all their wit, spirit, and ancestry to the table of learning. If I knew then what I know now, I'd a done anything I could to get Bernita over to Savannah State University that's down near to where we were from. They got some real smart folks over there. They full of love too. But God is everything and everything is God. What I'm saying is this. Bernita got just the lessons she needed. But more than that, she got some of her life back.

Cotty College was smack in the middle of nowhere, which was real nice for Bernita because she had room to think and grow. Them folks and that school were good to her and for her. Oh, there were a few people who saw her as a no-good nigger, riding on the benefits of being black. If any of them had bothered to sit down and talk to a black person, maybe they would have found out that the only benefit to being black was that it came with the instinct to survive. The sad part is, couldn't nobody call Bernita a name that was worse than what she was already used to hearing. Because of the way her family had treated her, it was easy for Bernita to put up with a few folks who hated themselves enough to turn they hate on her.

Bernita eventually went to school for social work, and after she graduated, moved up north to Wilmington, Delaware, and got the first job she put in for. She worked at one of those houses for women who been abused. Ain't life something? In a way she was taking care of a little piece of herself and the grandmother she never knew.

CHAPTER 5

reaping what you sow

When Bernita left for school my daddy died the very next day. His death made me think of an old joke Moms Mabley used to tell: "Don't talk about the dead unless its good. He's dead, good."

Me and Buster threw a home-going celebration that was more for us than it was for him. Only one of my other sisters came down, everybody else was there for the partying. My daddy didn't understand that he got to live long so he would have a chance to change his ways, but he never did. His mess got passed on to me and Buster 'cause like it or not, we was the closest to him. Now I didn't know any of this when I was alive, so I kept on living the way I always had.

I got a little place of my own, but Buster stayed right there in that house. I was feeling like I had been set free. There are folks who's very presence is like a weight on your life. Seems like when they die, you get to live. That's how it was when my daddy died.

I was running from one man to the next when one of them finally snagged me. He was everything I needed: love and life. But that life was short lived. I'm a tell you true, it's better to have a good love that's short lived than to have none at all.

I died about a year and a half after Bernita left to go to school, but that was not the end of me. No siree Bob. I been watching over Bernita since then.

I sure was lucky to have a niece, because she was my way to start all over again. The only problem was that she was making the same mistakes I made. But love always calls, and when it do, you better answer. I told you before that the unfulfilled longings of the ancestors are passed over to our children. Good thing I died when I did, 'cause that's when Bernita needed me most.

Everybody is meant to have love in their life. Love comes in many ways, times, and forms. Most often though, we ain't ready for it when it comes. We're usually too busy with the baggage of past hurts to run freely into the arms of love. It was a good thing for Bernita that I made my transition to the other side. Now what I'm about to say will sound strange at first, but then it will make all kinds of sense. Those of us who are over here on the other side love to meddle with the living. Not like in them crazy movies like *Poltergeist* or *Bones*. No sir, no ma'am. We don't meddle to cause fear and confusion. We do it to get in your business to set you on the right path. Now, I know that this ain't in line with what they call popular thinking. It ain't a field of study or nothing like that, but it's true. You think back on a time when you were head over heels in love with somebody who turned out to be all wrong. Now think on it harder and you'll remember that you got a strong feeling that something just wasn't right. Bingo! That was one of us meddling, trying to tell you that real love was right around the corner. Where do you think Luther Vandross got that song that says you gotta wait for love? That's right, he got it from us. We whispered it to him and he listened.

Now think on this. You ever see somebody, and you feel like they can be right for you even though you don't know anything about them. It's a real good feeling at first but then your head gets in the way. That's when you start to say, "Oh, but I'm kind of seeing somebody," or "He's not my type, "he doesn't make enough money." Maybe you've been hurt by somebody with the same name, or something like that so you make a bunch of excuses and just keep on running. I'm gonna tell you clear and loud, no matter how hard or fast you try to run, love is gonna find you. And when love calls, you better answer.

CHAPTER 6

killing kindness

You can do bad all by yourself.

—ANONYMOUS BLACK WOMAN

I guess my daddy, and the time Bernita spent at the home for beat-up women, made her run from any man who ever raised his voice. She didn't know many, but whenever a man even yelled at her to say, "Hi," from across the street or a passing car, Bernita would turn and go in another direction. One morning when she had been walking to work a beautiful man driving a delivery truck yelled out to tell her good morning. He slowed his truck down waiting for Bernita to say something back, but that girl never did. That young man had a big grin on his face when he first saw Bernita but when she didn't say nothing, it look to him like the sun stopped shining. Bernita just threw her head back and kept on walking like she was too good for him or something. She should've looked closer though, because what came next was the very thing Bernita should have run from.

Bernita couldn't tell it at the time, but Tyrone Phillip Thomas was gonna give her a beating that was worse than what me and her mama did. The only difference was, he wouldn't have to lay a hand on her.

Tyrone Phillip Thomas was what they call a pretty boy; the problem was he was way too old to be a boy. He loved himself something fierce. The day Bernita crossed the street from real love she ran smack into a big ole lie. Tyrone Phillip Thomas was on the lookout for a hard-working woman who cared less about her own needs than she did the needs of others.

"Hello," he said in a voice that really was buttery. "Are you alright, Miss, or is it Mrs.?"

"It's Miss, but um, my name is Bernita, Bernita Brown."

"Well, Miss Brown, so nice to meet you." The boy actually cooed when he talked. Then again so do pigeons, and just look at the mess they leave.

"Can I have the pleasure of walking with you?" Tyrone asked.

By now I was yelling from the other side, but Bernita ignored me like most folks do when they think they gonna get what they want.

Bernita really didn't know how to respond, but something from my first day in the park with her years before must have kicked in. She was liking the attention of Tyrone Phillip Thomas, just like I had liked the attention of that man with the big grin.

Ain't it a shame the way folks can remember the bad, but the good dies with them. I stole that from Shakespeare. Anyway, that boy talked just like he was *hot*. And he was, *a hot mess*.

"So Miss Brown, tell me why one as radiant as you is still a Miss?" It never occurs to men like Tyrone that some women actually choose to be single. In his mind, all single women were waiting for him.

"I just never got married; I work and, well, I stay busy." Bernita was acting like she didn't come from a family of women who knew how to say everything from "Get out of my face!" to "Baby, what you doing tonight?"

They walked the rest of the way to Passage Way House where Bernita worked. Bernita listened to Tyrone talk mainly about himself and the plans he had for his life and family. Tyrone had it all figured out: where he would live, how he would do it, and how perfect it all would be. All he needed was a wife and a bank that would understand the potential of his business plan. Bernita was what you'd call a level-headed woman, but when it comes to love, at some point all women get caught off-balance.

Tyrone met Bernita that day after work with a rose and the promise that he'd never be like the men who sent their wives to Passage Way House. "You are a queen, and you deserve to be treated as such," he said, like he really knew how kings treated their queens. They went to a little African restaurant where he ordered hot tea, but nothing else. Tyrone was acting as if the famine had found its way to the United States. The smells in the restaurant were like the ones that came from the shared kitchen Bernita had in college. Remember when I said that that first man made me think of them mashed sweet potatoes? Well, the mind sure is something powerful, but it's a trickster just the same. It can make you think you feeling one thing when you really thinking 'bout something else. Them smells in that restaurant put Bernita's mind back to them college days when she had a lot of love around her and she got confused into thinking that it was Tyrone and not her memories that were making her feel that way. Them smells got the best of her, and she suggested they order something.

Well, ole Tyrone said he was fasting, but that she could get something if she wanted to. Never one to offend, Bernita ignored the sounds coming from her belly, and kept listening to ole Tyrone's crooning.

"I have been on a fast for the past week," Tyrone said. "I felt that God was about to do something miraculous in my life, so I was preparing myself for it. It's only now that I know for certain what I've been getting ready for. It's you, Bernita Brown. I love you and it's you I've been waiting for."

I was yelling, "Run, Bernita run." She didn't wanna hear me, but I knew that my day would come.

Now Bernita wasn't dumb by no stretch of the imagination, but sometimes ignorance can take you down the same road. Which reminds me of something I meant to say earlier. Ignorance is only bliss to the person who came up with that saying.

Bernita did worry about Tyrone Phillip Thomas. She worried about why he wasn't looking for work until his proposed venture was approved, and she worried about how he supported himself. She worried about how he could fall so completely in love so quickly, as he had told her, when she didn't quite feel the same. But most of all, she worried if she was good enough for Tyrone.

Now most of Bernita's worry was me and the ancestors talking sense to her. But that last bit about not being good enough was all Tyrone. That boy had a way of making Bernita feel good, just so he could snatch that feeling away later on. He would say things like:

"You look good today. See, I told you that you would look better in a darker shade of lipstick. You gotta listen to me more."

Bernita got to thinking that whatever she did right, was all due to Tyrone.

There's something about evil that's just downright confident.

Now, you take Tyrone Phillip Thomas, here was a man who lived off of women like Bernita. He'd go from one to the other and sometimes juggle two or three at a time, never worrying about getting caught or hurt. Even when one of them women saw him for what he was, he'd convince them that they caused him to be unfaithful because they had no faith in him. Some people call them women stupid. When I was alive, I would have done the same, but stupid ain't got nothing to do with it.

Tyrone had made a rather comfortable living from the hardworking, decent women he went around with. When a man is running around on a whole lot of women, it ain't because he loves women so much that he can't get enough of them. As the French say, *"No compare."* The truth of the matter is some men don't really like women at all; they don't even like theyself.

Tyrone figured that he could keep on living like he'd been, but there was something about Bernita that made him want to slow down. Some folks have so much light in them that they can attract every and anything, but if that power ain't trained, it will pick up the first thing it shines on. Bernita had a glow that made everybody around her feel like they could do anything, but she wasn't aware of it. Some folks have charisma—you know, they have something in them that wins folks over. Well, that can be good, but it can also be bad. Now, I know some folks think that you attract what you need to work out. But listen to me closely. Most times folks are attracted to what they know they lack. When Tyrone met Bernita, he saw a power that he wished he had, and he wanted that power for himself.

the outcome is better than what you go through

I've sung a lot of songs and made some bad rhymes.

—LEON RUSSELL

After a year of reeling Bernita in and then pushing her away, Tyrone Phillip Thomas made Bernita feel like he was definitely better than she deserved. When he got her where he wanted her, he told her that they would be getting married. The marriage proposal was more like what they call a business proposition. That man was something else!

Mr. Tyrone Phillip Thomas had shut Bernita out the whole month leading up to his so-called proposal. He hadn't called her once and wouldn't answer her calls. She tried to contact him on the computer that she paid for but he wouldn't answer her e-mails. But his month of punishment had been my time to work. See, all a good life needs is a willing partner. Just because me and Bernita weren't in direct contact, so to speak, didn't mean that I couldn't be useful someplace else. You remember that boy that said "hi" to Bernita on the same day she met Tyrone; the one who drove the delivery truck? He was full of light. Well, it turns out that he had a lot more going for him than ole Tyrone did. The same day and the same way that I was hanging around Bernita, that young man had one of his ancestors around him. The ancestor's name was John Ray. I call him Ray from Around the Way. The young man was his son that he had been watching over. I found out that the boy's name was Douglas and that he felt a whole lot more for Bernita than she did for him. Douglas drove off from her that day feeling sad, but he didn't really know why. He had been rejected many times, but it never felt like this. Bernita's refusal was like a stab in his heart. I had a good conversation with Douglas's father, and we came up with a plan.

John Ray from Around the Way saw the hurt in his boy's heart just like I saw the emptiness in Bernita's. We got together and got in touch with them. Not directly, neither one of them was ready for that. We used television. Now I know that this is sounding stranger by the minute, but if you stop and think about it, you'll see that all of this lines up. Every now and then, you may notice that when you're watching TV, there will be something said that don't make a lick of sense, then all of a sudden, seem like sense is coming from out of nowhere. Well, that's us ancestors. We use television like it's a telephone. There are messages in everything. Nature is full of them. But more and more, as folks have turned away from nature, we have had to find other ways to get our points across.

Now some shows and television people are easier to use than others. So me and old John Ray got to talking through a guest on one of them talk shows. The woman was going on about finding the love you need.

"Love is all around you, you just need to tap into it and be specific. . . ." She was saying all of this like she thought it up herself.

"Write a letter to the person you will someday love. Write it just like you know who they are. Allow the letter, or letters, to speak your true heart. And if that doesn't work . . . "

By now, me and John Ray had got our point across. So we left the TV woman to whatever else she wanted to say.

"Try a dating service," she said. "They are very successful at making matches."

That man who was interviewing her looked at that woman like she sure was crazy.

"So, let me get this straight." He said, "Write a letter, and if that doesn't work, use a dating service?"

"Letter?" The woman from TV was looking like she had come out of some kind of trance, and I guess she had. "What letter? No, I said a dating service. That's better."

John Ray from Around the Way was cracking up. We had done what we set out to do. Bernita and Douglas had both been watching the television show. Douglas sat down and commenced to writing just like we knew he would.

Dear Wife,

You don't know me. I hardly know myself. My name is Douglas Ford. I heard in a television show that I should write to the person I want to meet. I'm not quite sure why I'm writing this, but it makes sense. I love you. What I mean is, I want to love you. I have been on my own for most of my life and I don't want to be like this anymore. Most people think that I am just a loner, but I would rather be that person who is in the center of things. I just don't know how.

Well, I just want to say that you are / will be all that I hope you are. You are beautiful, kind, and loving. You can see the good in others, even when they can't see it themselves. You love music, art, and the things I also find important. You may be a good cook, but that doesn't matter because I'm a great one, if I do say so myself. You make me feel like I am in the center of things. And when we make love, it feels like we have always been together. You satisfy me in ways that I could not have imagined. You complete me in the areas that I thought were just fine. We walk well together and I love you.

Your love,

Douglas

I saw that boy write that letter and I got so tickled, I didn't know what to do. Life is a fascinating thing. You can meet someone and see them just for a short moment, and in that moment, they can make a bigger impression than someone you've known your whole lifetime.

Well, Bernita was in her own home, and she heard them planted thoughts of ours too, but the thing that was sending Douglas in the right direction, was sending Bernita down the wrong path.

Dear Husband,

I know that you are my love, but for some reason, you cannot commit yourself to me. I guess that I am mainly responsible for this. I have a hard time allowing myself to lose control. What I am trying to say is, you are so in charge of things, and I am sure that you will be good for me. But it's hard for me to let you take charge. I want to be loved and to give you my love. I hope that someday,

*I can give you this letter. You are my dream love. You are beauti-
ful, kind, wonderful, and caring. You are smart and I know that
I am lucky to be around you.*

I love you.

Your wife for life,
Bernita

That girl always did like a rhyme. Anyway, if it's trouble you're
looking for, then it's trouble you're going to get. As soon as she got
done writing that letter, ole you know who called. None other than
Tyrone Phillip Thomas, himself.

You ever notice that right when you ready to get over somebody that's wrong for you, then here they come acting like they all
right? Well, when Tyrone did call, it was 3:00 in the morning.
Bernita was so happy and relieved to hear his voice she had forgotten what she told herself just one day before. Bernita was trying to get over Tyrone Phillip Thomas and move on with her life.
She had listened to enough battered women to know that what
Tyrone was doing was a form of abuse.

"Bernita, hey girl," he said to her over the phone in the wee
hours that morning. He called her from one of those cellular
phones that another woman was paying for. He'd told Bernita that
the woman was just a friend who wanted to invest in his business.
Funny thing is, he told the other woman the same thing about
Bernita when she found Bernita's name on the title of the car that
he was driving.

"Bernita," he said, "I know you love me, and you know that I
feel the same. Well, I can't be apart from you no more. I been trying to wait for my business to get off the ground, but I'm afraid
that if I wait any longer, I might lose you. So I think you should

marry me now so we can be together and support each other in our dreams."

I had to give it to old Tyrone. He was a hell of a lot smarter than them old dogs I ran 'round with. Bernita was half asleep so Tyrone caught her off guard. Plus, she had just written that letter and then he called. Bernita knew that there was no such thing as a coincidence, so she decided that it was fate. Well, Bernita was right on one count, but real wrong on the other. Tyrone's call was *not* a coincidence, but that didn't mean that it was meant to play out the way it did. Bernita had a choice in the matter. She chose wrong.

Well, she commenced to crying, and when Tyrone asked her why, she told him that she was all mixed up.

"I'm happy, but I'm scared too. Where have you been? I was afraid that something had happened to you, since I haven't heard from you for so long. I thought you ran off with somebody else and I was mad. So I had just given up. Now you say you want to marry me." Tyrone knew the power of silence, so for a good while he didn't say nothing. When he did, he was true to form.

"Bernita Brown," he said real slow, "please tell me that you are the same woman that I have spent the last month praying and fasting over. Please tell me that what I feel in my heart is true. Please don't make me and God a liar. You know me better than anyone in the world," he said.

If Bernita had been listening with her head instead of a heart that had been broken, she'd a known that Tyrone wasn't none of what she wrote in that letter.

"I know that you are the one for me and that I am the only man for you. I wish I had more to offer in the way of financial security, but you're not rich either."

You ever notice that folks who try to trick you into something with flattery always end up insulting you instead? If you listen past all them pretty words, you'll realize that whatever they say comes back to what you can do for them and not the other way around. Like Michael Jackson's baby sister say, "What have you done for me lately?" (I bet you didn't even know that I was so hip. Just 'cause you dead, don't mean you ain't up on things.)

Anyways, that man went on to tell Bernita that they could really build a life together and do all the things he saw in his visions. Tyrone told her that they could build a business together and she wouldn't have to listen to the whining women at the shelter no more; they could work together. Bernita had never complained about her job, she loved that she could help women who were in trouble. It was Tyrone who thought her job was less than what it was.

Tyrone told Bernita a whole bunch of mess until he finally stumbled on something close to what she wanted to hear.

"Bernita baby, please say yes. I want you to be the mother of my children. Then we can show the world what a loving family looks like."

Well, with that Tyrone Phillip Thomas hit bingo right down the middle. Bernita didn't just want children, she wanted to give love to a child in a way that she hadn't been loved. She thought that loving someone would give her back the childhood she didn't have. Bernita had never told a soul, but in her mind, she had decorated her children's rooms from the time they was babies on up to when they would leave for college.

Well Tyrone got Bernita right where she lived with all that talk about showing the world what a family should be. Bernita didn't need to show the world, but she dearly wanted a family.

Well, Bernita managed to get out a defeated "yes." Tyrone

Phillip Thomas went on and planned their wedding. It was more fancy than Bernita could afford, but that didn't stop Tyrone none. No sir, nothing was too good for his Bernita, especially since she was paying. True to his plan, Tyrone made the wedding day pretty as a picture. But all the money and planning in the world couldn't have made that wedding into a marriage. It was a bigger lie than even I would've been prepared for.

One day a little more than a year into the marriage, when Bernita was growing more disappointed in herself than she was in Tyrone, she came home earlier than usual. She wasn't feeling well, and one of her co-workers made her go home to rest.

"I don't like the way you looking, B," she said. "You look like you 'bout to fall over."

Bernita took her friend's advice and dragged herself home to rest. Things weren't that good with her and Tyrone. Let me back up a bit so you can get to what I'm telling you. Bernita had never made love to nobody before Tyrone and it was a full month into the marriage before they did. When they finally did get down to business, it was as clumsy as my first time in the park. The only difference was that at least the man with the big grin told me nice things, even if he was lying. Tyrone knew that it was Bernita's first time, but he ain't do nothing to make it special. "Today's the day, Bernie." From the day they got married he had taken to calling her Bernie. She was the only girl in my daddy's house that even got to have a girl's name and here Tyrone come along turning it into one for a boy. Bernita didn't like it at all, but she didn't even know why. Once she tried to correct Tyrone and told him that she really did prefer Bernita. She told him that her friends sometimes called her B. She didn't mind that at all, but she didn't like the feel of Bernie. Well, Tyrone made her believe that it was his way to show his love.

"That's my pet name for you," he said. "Only I can call you that." She didn't like it, but Bernita went on and put up with it anyway.

"Today's the day for what?" Bernita was hoping she knew what Tyrone meant. Tyrone figured that if he held Bernita off long enough, he could do the same thing he had been doing: make her feel privileged just to be near him. Well, on that first time with Tyrone, he told her to take off all her clothes and to lie down. When Bernita told him she was too shy and that maybe he could take them off for her, Tyrone turned to walk out of the little bedroom that Bernita had made so nice.

"Wait," she was calling after him. "Please don't leave, I just haven't done this before."

"That's right," Tyrone said, "you haven't. You don't know what to do but you don't want me to tell you either."

Bernita was trying to tell Tyrone how she was feeling embarrassed, but listening was not one of Tyrone's talents.

"Maybe we should just wait until you're ready for this." Right when Bernita was about to recognize the stories she heard at work, old Tyrone switched up on her.

"I want you to be ready, Bernie. I only waited this long for you to get comfortable. I thought you were ready; please forgive me."

The boy had been acting his whole life, but his performance that day should have gotten some kind of NAACP Image Award or something. Well, by the time he got done with my niece, she was begging him to make love to her. Once she had her clothes off and she was on the bed, he pulled back the covers she was hiding under, pulled a chair up to the side of the bed, and sat there staring. When Bernita got up the nerve to ask what he was doing, he told her that he was taking her into himself. Now, mind you, he still had on all of his clothes. The first thing captors do to prisoners is to strip them naked. The first thing Adam said when he got a hold of a piece of fruit from the tree of knowledge was "I'm naked." Somewhere in our nakedness we begin to feel like it's our soul that's uncovered, and that's as far from the truth as Tyrone was from treating Bernita with any kindness. After a while he climbed on top of her, put himself inside, and got his own relief. Now ain't no sense in telling one side of a story and acting like it's whole, but Bernita is my blood, my life, so that's the story I'm telling. True enough though, Tyrone became a part of me when he became a part of her. To say that Tyrone got relief is not giving you the whole picture. He had a physical release, but wasn't no more joy in it for him than it was for her.

Tyrone Phillip Thomas went through a lot of women, because what he really wanted was another man. You can cast all the stones you want, but in the end you going to find out like I did that what we do, and who we do it with, is not who we are. The problem with Tyrone Phillip Thomas was not the fact that he's homosexual, no sir, no ma'am. It was that he hides who he is from himself. Every man, woman, and child wants to be loved, but you got to get the love you need.

Tyrone had been teased about being "that way" before he even knew what "that way" was. He had learned to hide his desires from everybody including his self. When you hide who you are, you are heading straight toward trouble, but eventually that trouble is gonna be turned on everybody around you.

Well, to make this long story a little less long, that day when she wasn't feeling well, Bernita walked in on Tyrone making love to another man. When she came into the apartment, she could hear sounds of love that Tyrone never made with her.

"Yes, you are wonderful. This feels so good. I need you so bad."

Well, Bernita thought it was another woman and immediately saw herself to blame. "I'm not passionate enough. I'm ugly. I'm skinny." All of the things Tyrone had told her in the time they were together had now become ideas of her own about herself. Bernita was too afraid to walk in on Tyrone, but she couldn't move from the place outside the bedroom door either. I know what it means to have the wind knocked out of you. That's how it was for me the day I died. The wind just went out from me. Bernita felt like that too, but she was still alive. At least her body was. That day Tyrone did something to her spirit that just about killed that poor child. Sometimes though, it seems like stuff keeps happening to us, when its really happening *for* us. It says in the Bible that all things work together for the good of them who love God and are called according to God's plan. Bernita had no way of knowing this, but the thing that was going on behind that door was happening for her. Bernita slid down the wall across from that bedroom door and sat right there until Tyrone and his plaything came out.

When they did, Bernita's sadness turned to shock, shock turned to rage, and rage turned into madness. The plaything was a man and he was even prettier than Pretty Boy Tyrone. When Tyrone saw Bernita his man commenced to screaming like he was the one to walk in on her.

"You said she was gone, that you were through with her. How could you do this to me? I hate you Tyrone, I hate you." He was yelling at the top of his height, which was about six foot five.

"Oh Lord, look what you've done," Tyrone moaned but you couldn't tell if he was talking to the Lord, or Bernita. "Why me? Why, Lord?"

In all this commotion, Bernita chose to remain silent. She had no idea that her silence was her strength. For a moment, she thought she couldn't talk. But there are times, and this was one, that having nothing to say is more powerful than anything said. Well, Tyrone's friend ran out the door still screaming while Tyrone was still talking 'bout "why me?" Bernita finally pulled herself up from where she was sitting. She was dizzy at first, but she found enough strength to help her stand. Now, I told you that Mrs. Morris kept her word and was watching over Bernita. What you also need to know is that when you need it the most, you can call on your memories to help you through. People who see ghosts everywhere need to stop conjuring. It's the memory of the spirit that lives on, good or bad. Well, Bernita needed strength and she thought about Mrs. Morris and her husband showing her love. Right then she heard Mrs. Morris say, "You deserve to be happy, you deserve to be loved."

"I deserve to be happy. I deserve to be loved," Bernita said through her tears. She said it over and over and me and Anna Louise were chanting it right after her.

Tyrone thought Bernita had lost her mind, but she was just getting it back.

Bernita left Tyrone the same way she left our little house on C Street. She went back for a few belongings and to set things straight with her landlord. She actually paid out the last three months on her lease. She didn't have to tell the landlord her business 'cause he watched everything and saw most of what went on in his building. He felt for Bernita, but didn't want her to feel no extra shame. So he took the check, thanked her, and told her not to worry 'cause the outcome was always better than the stuff you have to go through.

CHAPTER 8

set yourself free

Sometimes if you try to hold on to somebody, you have to stand there and watch them.

—AUNT BABE

You ever notice when you finally get tired of walking around in a mess, and you try to move on, you find that mess is still clinging to you? That's what happened to Bernita. She left Tyrone in a rent-free place where he could do whatever he wanted to, for three more months anyway. But that's just when he decided that what he wanted was to be with Bernita. He tried everything. He told her lies about the man she caught him with, how he was blackmailing him into doing things he didn't want to do. When that didn't work, he lied and said he had been raped when he was young and now as a result, he was sometimes confused. He said that she of all people should understand this since many of the women she helped were so used to abuse, that they chose it over and over again. Bernita politely asked him to tell his own story and to leave others alone. She also told him to be who he was. Well,

Tyrone had the nerve to say that he wasn't gay and that he had only been with a man that one time and it was probably because she was so frigid.

I was proud of Bernita because she reached back and pulled on the strength of her ancestors again and found out what she was made of. "I'm not a part of what you did or who you did it with," she said as calm as a river after a storm; on the surface it's smooth like glass, but underneath all kinds of things are going on.

"I left you because you don't love me or anyone else. You don't even love yourself. I have to find my life the same way you need to find yours." Then she hung up the phone. It kept ringing all night, and she let it. The next day she changed the number as easy as if she was changing socks.

That's when I started whispering to Bernita again. See, when you erase a bad story you gotta write another one, or else that old story gonna keep coming back to you. This time I used the radio to get to Bernita. Now you can believe me if you want, that's up to you. Music does more than soothe the soul; it brings balance to the mind, body, and spirit. Pay close attention the next time your clock radio jumps on and listen to what is singing at you. Chances are you'll hear ancestral messages all up in it.

That night when Bernita tried to calm herself down on account of she wasn't that used to telling nobody off, she went looking through her old music to find something that would give her some peace. She searched through her neatly organized stacks of CDs and found the one she was looking for. It was an old Phoebe Snow song called "No Regrets." Just listening to Phoebe will tell you that she's an old soul who knows a lot more than her years let on. "No Regrets" is this upbeat, happy-sounding song, but just as soon as you get caught up in that happy tune, you realize that the woman is saying that she ain't taking no more mess and that she ain't got no regrets for nothing.

Now if Billie Holiday or Betty Carter had sung that song, it would've took you in a whole other direction. Mind you, Billie and Betty sure do have a place in my heart, but since my Bernita was of a different time, her sad song needed a different beat. Rap music ain't that far from the blues. If you listen close you'll hear some of the same things. Anyway, Bernita was just about to put Phoebe in the CD player and that's right when I put the radio to work. Lalah Hathaway's and Joe Sample's tune came on real loud and sudden and Bernita had to stop and listen. "When Your Life Was Low" was the tune Bernita truly needed. Well, Joe got together with Lalah and painted a picture that just has to be heard. Their song talks about a person who done propped somebody else up just like my Bernita did. After a while that propped-up person got to thinking that they were too good for the one who done helped them, and went on they way like they never needed no help. But that's all right with Lalah, 'cause as she says, that man sure did love her when his life was low.

Bernita heard that song and her back went straight. She sat up tall and got to thinking about how she had propped up Tyrone. She was just about to get mad when I put Donnie McClurkin on that radio. He was talking about how we all fall down, but we have to get back up. Well, Bernita thought back to the day she sat down and wrote a letter to the husband she hoped to meet and how she got to thinking that that person was Tyrone. She looked through her things and found that letter. Mind you, it didn't take too long on account of Bernita is so organized. Well, she read that letter and just cried. She could see that she had written from her true heart, but she pinned her hopes on something that was false.

Old folks used to say, "Be careful what you ask for, 'cause you just might get it." But I say, be careful with getting things that look a lot like the thing you asked for, 'cause it's hard to get rid of them.

Back when Bernita wrote that letter, she had been looking for a place to put her broken heart and she thought Tyrone was the pillow she needed to rest on. Well, Bernita got done reading that first letter and sat down to write another one. Just when she was about to write, the radio DJ got to talking. Well, it was really me, but he ain't know that.

"That was Lalah Hathaway and Joe Sample followed by Donnie McClurkin, reminding us that no matter how bad we feel after a breakup, love is still possible. And I hope that the woman who just left me knows that I'm the one who helped her when she needed it."

Now I didn't tell him to say that last part, but I got my point in just the same! Bernita sat down to write a letter, and to my joy, she wrote it to Tyrone.

Dear Tyrone,

I am truly sorry that things did not work out for us. I did everything I could to make you love me. But now I see that what I really needed was for me to love myself. I really can't blame you for any feelings of loss or emptiness. Those are the feelings that I chose. I didn't want them, but I chose them just the same. There were many times when I felt that things were not right between us. I somehow believed that if I worked harder, everything would be all right. I had forgotten something that I heard long ago: "In love, the two are to become one." I could not work out our problems on my own. I needed you to work them out with me. That would require that you be willing to work. But you, my dear Tyrone,

were not. You had a hidden agenda all along. The funny thing is
that your real agenda was hidden from you. You are afraid to be
who you are, but even more afraid to be what you are. I don't
blame you. A life lived in fear is to be feared.

Well, dear Tyrone, I will not send this letter to you. I don't need
to. I simply had to let myself know that I can't feel sorry for the
things you caused but refuse to see. I wish you well.

Bernita

Now, to say that I was proud would be like saying James Brown can get down. I got the joy that you get when you glad to see that somebody is doing something that you should've done. The joy wasn't a feeling, it was more of a knowing.

After Bernita wrote that letter to Tyrone, she wrote one to the person that would be her real love.

Dear Love,

I don't know who you are, but I sure wish I did. That way, I
would have someone to share my feelings with. I have a great need
to love and be loved. I read somewhere that when the student is
ready, the teacher appears. I guess it's the same way with love. I
want you to know that life is preparing me for you. My journey to
you has not been easy, but I feel that somehow it will be worth it.
Someday I will be able to thank you for what I am becoming. Un-
til then I will learn to love on my own.

Your true love, Bernita

Well, I was just beaming like the morning sun when I got to knowing that over on the other side of town my friend Ray from Around the Way was talking to his fine son Douglas Ford. Now remember, I could look in on him from time to time because of that one little contact he made with Bernita. Ray from Around the Way had been a ladies' man all his life. If things were at all fair, I guess I would have been called a men's lady. Anyway, Ray didn't know his son, he didn't even know that he had one named Douglas 'till he passed on over. In some ways that's a real shame, but in others it's a real blessing. If you try even a little to live right, even your bad will work out for your good. Douglas turned out to be a better man than his father 'cause his father could be a father from the other side. Death is a blessing. At least it is for everybody over on this side. It's real hard on the ones who been left behind, but that's because they think of it as being left. Truth is, the connection only gets stronger.

"Don't leave me, don't leave me." Folks be just crying at the funeral.

What most folks don't know is, we dead are even more present than before. When you get to thinking on us and remembering who we are, it brings us closer and makes us more powerful than we were in life. That's why you always see a bunch of old folks sitting around after the funeral telling funny stories and laughing. Sometimes they get drunk and laugh all night. They just old enough to remember how their parents and grandparents did funerals and they close enough to death to see that everything is gonna be all right.

Anyway, what I'm saying is, just 'cause Ray didn't know his son in life don't mean that he couldn't get in touch after death. Now, Ray had more kids than any three women, but in death he made sure that he got around to check on all of them. He paid real close attention to Douglas though, 'cause he was special. Douglas's mama died when he was still a young boy. Ray was still alive then but he didn't know about Douglas, so the boy ended up with an aunt who didn't really want him. He and Bernita had more in common than two peas out of the same pod. Douglas's aunt told him that she didn't want him, but that she would do what she could. That's just about how I felt about Bernita. Truth be told, both of us could've done a whole lot more. Douglas's aunt didn't have any other children, so there wasn't anybody for Douglas to talk to neither. She never allowed him to run the streets, as she called it, or play like most other kids did. Douglas took to drawing the things he wanted to do. Art was his way to escape. When Douglas got to high school, he had a teacher who noticed his work. She made him feel like he could be an artist, but she didn't really know how to help. Douglas didn't get good grades in nothing but art. Wasn't nobody she knew giving black boys money to go to school for that. If he had learned to play ball, things could have been different.

Well, Douglas got to believing he could do art, anyway. When his aunt asked him what his plans were now that he was a man, he told her that he was gonna be an artist. She laughed at him and put him out in the streets. Wasn't too many people trying to feel for this average kid who painted pretty pictures.

So, Douglas had to learn to make his own way real fast. He took all kinds of jobs and got a spare room in a rooming house. After he got the delivery job, he got a little apartment. Douglas was working, going to school, and painting the way he liked. One of the teachers at the college saw some talent and made him feel real good about the pictures he made. She has been helping Douglas to sell his work and now more and more folks are taking notice. Douglas is afraid to step all the way into his art on account of what his aunt said and did. All things have a way of working out for the good. If he didn't keep that delivery job, he would not have seen Bernita. If he hadn't seen Bernita, then I wouldn't have seen Ray, and we couldn't do what we got to do. You catch my drift? Everything is connected to everything else. Whenever Ray was around Douglas, I could sense it. 'Cause in a way, he was around my Bernita too. Douglas wasn't like his daddy in the love department. Just like Bernita had learned to pour herself into her work and helping other people, Douglas put himself into his true purpose. That boy was something special for sure. He started driving that delivery truck to make one end meet the other, but he started painting so he could breathe. He was good too. Douglas and Bernita had other things in common—just like her, he didn't have a lot of love growing up, so he was afraid to really go after the kind of love he needed. Douglas didn't know much more about life and love than Bernita did, but if me and Ray got our way, they were gonna get all that they needed.

That day had been a tough one for Douglas. He had been seeing a young woman who he thought he loved. She said she loved him too, but on this particular day, she came over to where he lived to tell him that she had been seeing someone else and that she was leaving town and getting married. Douglas was more than hurt. It had been hard for him to open up to anybody, and when he finally did, it was always the wrong one. Women ain't the only ones who get hurt in love. Most of the men we call dogs had some help becoming one. Some men get hurt by love and get so lost that they have to turn that hurt on whoever it is that tries to love them again. That's what was happening with Douglas when Ray went to him and told him to give love a chance. Now if you ever want a real close visit with the ancestors, go to a good bookstore. Most good writers know that when they honor the ancestors with their lives, we honor them with our stories.

Douglas had to make a delivery to one of the biggest black bookstore chains. One of the owners of Karibou Bookstore, Brother Simba, had been waiting for a shipment of Alice Walker's latest book. He was standing in the doorway when Douglas drove up.

"This will not be a quick trip my brother, so pull around back and bring the books in that way." Brother Simba had been dealing in books for a long time along with his partner Brother Yao. They were purposeful and conscious men, the kind you folks down there need more of. When Simba and Yao opened the first Karibou Bookstore, the ancestors hovered around Karibou like moths to a bare bulb and helped them open four more stores to boot. Simba and Yao didn't play when it came to their books and their authors; all good authors were "their authors."

They hosted parties and book signings for the best and the brightest, and because they were truly blessed, they made sure that whoever they came in contact with who wanted to read had a chance to. Simba and Yao secretly donated money and books to just about every cause in town. The people who knew them were aware that they were on point and generous, but they would be surprised by just how far their power and pull could go.

"You got the books?" Simba yelled to Douglas before he could even get out of his truck. Douglas respected Brother Simba from the first time he met him. Simba was tough, but Douglas could tell he had a good heart, and Douglas admired his struggle to keep black folks reading, and black authors in business.

"I know they got you on a schedule, but you need to come in and check out the store."

As Douglas walked into Karibou, he admired the rows of books and the artfully designed store. Just as he was reaching for a book, another one fell off the shelf. Well, it didn't really fall, Ray and I actually pushed it. Sometimes you have to help a brother out, and that boy sure nuff needed to have that book in his life. It was called *A Love No Less* and it was a collection of African-American love stories collected over two hundred years. When Douglas reached down to pick it up, without knowing why, he decided to buy it and approached the register. "No, man," Simba said, "that's our gift to you for all your hard work."

As Douglas reached over to shake Simba's hand, Brother Simba, ever serious, said, "Yo, man. Don't forget about my Chester Higgins books. Make me your first stop."

Douglas left the shop and when he got out to his truck he had no idea why he'd bought that book. His head was swimming, as they say, but if you ask me, it ain't the head that's swimming, it's the heart. But that's a conversation for another time.

When Douglas got home he read most of that book that night, love letter after love letter. Some letters were real old and were written by slaves, others were written while folk were at war, and others were written more recently. As he turned page after page he yearned for the kind of love he found in that book.

Around 3:30 A.M., Douglas put the book down and decided to write.

Dear Love,

There are those who say that true love does not exist. That there is no such thing as a soul mate. They don't know the love of black folks. Our love is pure soul. We love so much that we have a need to keep going back for more, even when love bites us in the you know where. I am writing this letter to prove to those who don't believe that true love is real. I am writing this letter now, before

I meet you, to prove that when we do meet, we will know it. It may take a while, and it may not, but we will be as one. I have read about the love of those who had to endure slavery, Jim Crow, beatings, lynching, and worse, yet love remained. I am having a hard time finding you, my love, but I know that I will. I feel, correction, I know that when I find me, I will find you. Walking with you will be like looking in a mirror. I look forward to our love and to showing others that our souls are connected.

Your true love,
Douglas

CHAPTER 9

back in love again

If you can't love the one you're with, find the one you love.

—AUNT BABE

Why do bad men happen to good women? That sure is a good question, and it's relevant, 'cause when Bernita left Tyrone she fell out of the George Foreman grill and into the fire.

Most people think that they can leave a bad relationship behind. But that ain't always the way life is. Not only do you bring that bad with you, you use it to gauge what to do and who to do it with. The same thing happened to Bernita. She thought she just happened to meet the next man, Jimmymack (that's his real name, no lie). What really happened was she picked him out of a lineup of men who she thought to be least like old Tyrone Phillip Thomas. That's what I mean about using the old as a measuring stick for the new. Where Tyrone was a pretty boy, Jimmymack was rough and rugged. Had it not been for his big old laugh, he would have been downright hard to look at.

Jimmymack sure could laugh though. His laugh made you look past the big nose that didn't go with his little squinty eyes. He had big lips too, but not the kind that made you think of soft clouds or proud Africans. No ma'am, no sir, Jimmymack's lips ran right up into his nose or maybe his nose ran into his lips. Anyway, what Jimmymack did have besides that laugh was a body. He had broad shoulders and strong arms and thighs. His waist made you want to wrap your arms around it and leave them there. He was tall and muscular with a stomach that looked like he did sit-ups all day and night. If you saw Jimmymack from behind, you might have thought that one of them Greek gods had fallen down to earth and been dipped in Hershey's chocolate. But Lord, when he turned around you'd know otherwise. Jimmymack wasn't just hard on the eyes, except for his laugh he was also hard in his manner. But I guess that Bernita was making sure that she got as far away from Tyrone Phillip Thomas as she could. Jimmymack loved him some "Bernisha." That's what he called her 'cause he talked funny too. I think his lips got in the way of his words.

He loved Bernita so hard, that he didn't want to let her go. He hated when she left his apartment for work. "Why can't you just stay here?" he would say all loud and hard. "My place ain't cute like yours but this is where I want you when I gets home." Bernita mistook all his roughhousing for love.

One day he came by her job to pick her up. She was spending too much time with them crazy dykes, he told her. He didn't like where she worked. Said it was too dangerous over there with crazy women who had even crazier men looking for them. The day he banged on the front door everyone thought it was a husband or boyfriend looking for their woman. MaBisha Moore, Bernita's secretary and friend, opened the door to see who it was.

Bernita loved MaBisha from the first day she met her. MaBisha came to the shelter late one night after her husband had beat her and broken her down. When Bernita saw her the next morning though, MaBisha was laughing with a group of women. "My arm is broke. It'll mend, but he ain't never gonna pee straight again." Bernita went and looked over MaBisha's paperwork and then took her into her little office to ask her some questions. Behind closed doors without a crowd, MaBisha wasn't as tough as she made herself out to be.

"I loved that man something bad," she told Bernita. "All I got to show for it is a heart full of pain."

MaBisha cried and Bernita held her. Something about Ma-Bisha reminded Bernita of her mother, all tough on the outside but crying on the inside. Unlike Buster, MaBisha took to love like a snake takes to tall grass. Bernita filled out what's called an intake form and MaBisha has been around ever since. She didn't stay at the shelter as a resident for too long. She got out and found an apartment for herself and her four children. She had a job, but she volunteered at Passage Way House on weekends and sometimes weeknights. Her youngest child was fifteen and the rest went up to eighteen. She could leave them at home without much worry. Unlike her husband, her kids knew how to behave. She did so much to make the other women feel better that it just made sense for her to work there, so Bernita hired her fulltime at Passage Ways.

"How can I help you?" MaBisha said to Jimmymack the day he came looking for Bernita. MaBisha had an I-don't-care delivery that went with a get-from-'round-my-door look. MaBisha kept one hand on the locked screen door. She had learned from experience that some men would just rip a screen door right off the little latch to prove how much they loved their wife.

"I'm looking for Bernisha, she works here." Now, MaBisha had figured this man had to be the one and only Jimmymack. He called more than he should have so she recognized his voice from all the times she had to tell him that Bernita was in a session.

"May I take a message?" she would ask in her I-really-don't-want-to-but-I-will-anyway tone. She was good on the phone and working the door. Believe me when I tell you that even a bitter woman has a place in this world. All they gotta do is find it.

"This is Jimmymack," he would say on the phone.

He would slur his words like he was just learning to talk. Now, I been through more men than Bernita has even introduced herself to, but ain't nothing about Jimmymack that would have turned my head. It's only 'cause I've crossed to the other side that I can even know why she was with him.

"Tell her to call me if she wants to but if she don't, uh, dat's fine too."

MaBisha didn't have the luxury of sitting high and looking low like I do, so she asked Bernita just what she saw in Jimmymack.

"How did you meet him?" she asked her. "And why didn't you run fast in the other direction when you met him?"

MaBisha never held back what she was thinking, and there are times when you need a MaBisha in your corner.

"You wouldn't believe me if I told you," Bernita said. Now, when folks decide that you ain't gonna believe them, get ready not to. "I met him after I got divorced."

"I knew that." MaBisha didn't want the long version. She wanted quick truth. "Get to it," she told Bernita.

"I met him the day my divorce was final. I took the bus to and from court. Tyrone wanted to keep the car that I bought and I didn't want that mess to drag out no more than it did, so I let him have it. On the way back from court I met Jimmymack on the bus."

"So he ain't got no car either. I guess y'all do have something in common." MaBisha really did mean to be funny, but she was the only one laughing.

"He has a car," Bernita told her. She wasn't even grinning.

"Don't tell me it's in the shop, or did he loan it to his brother and the brother got it stolen?"

"He was driving the bus. Do you want me to tell this story or do you want to tell it?" For Bernita, that was sassy.

MaBisha really got to laughing now. "That's all right, girl. I ain't got enough imagination for where this story is going."

"Jimmymack is a bus driver, but he goes to night school. He's studying to be a pastry chef. He really is a good guy, you just gotta get to know him."

"Or figure out what he's saying." MaBisha stood up from where she was sitting and Bernita could tell that she was getting ready to preach or to leave. Either way, there was gonna be drama involved.

"Now I am not one to look down or up at somebody just 'cause of a job," MaBisha said. "And if you say he's a good man, well, then I believe it.

"But I'm a tell you the truth, that man is rough with what he say and what he don't say. He is one of those men that make you feel sorry for him 'cause he only got you to love. Then after a while, you find out that there's a reason he only got you. Make sure you watch him closely." MaBisha paused and looked at Bernita. She softened her tone, but only by a little.

"Being hurt by love don't make you bad, Bernita, it just make you sad. But don't run from a dog over to a wolf."

Sometimes when somebody gets a healing it can heal everything and anybody around them. MaBisha was talking from the truth and the light that Bernita had helped her see. Now, she was shining that light back on Bernita. God got a way of putting folks in your path so you can help them to help you. Most times we miss the very help we need, 'cause we don't give it when we should.

On the day Jimmymack came banging on her work door, Bernita remembered what MaBisha had told her a few months before. She had been paying close attention, and just as her friend had said, Jimmymack was holding on to her tighter and tighter. When she had relaxed enough to do what she thought was making love, Jimmymack had her hooked. He was a real passionate lover. He made Bernita feel more beautiful than Tyrone had made her feel ugly. But comparisons ain't never good when the ruler you're using to measure with is broke. Jimmymack made Bernita feel wanted and needed. So much so that she got to thinking that love was need.

On the day that Jimmymack came to the office, MaBisha was trying to figure out if she should tell Bernita that he was outside. MaBisha had had so much trouble in her life that she developed a radar that picked up on it when it was coming. Most folks choose to ignore it, but MaBisha decided after she started working at Passage Way to make it her business to pay close attention.

Bernita just happened to hear Jimmymack out there trying to talk so she rushed into the mess that MaBisha was trying to keep her from.

"Hey, Jimmymack." Bernita was being all cheery like folks do when they trying to get you to do the same. Jimmymack didn't know that trick. He just got louder.

"Why she acting like she your woman or something? Can't I come get you and give you a ride home? Can't I?"

"Jimmy, keep your voice down. This is where I work."

"I know that, so why she acting like you ain't here? And I told you my name is Jimmymack. It's all one name. Why you keep fronting me in front of these people? You coming out or what?"

"Bernita's not leaving and neither am I," MaBisha said.

Bernita was more embarrassed than she was mad and that's a shame. The Bible tells you to get angry but don't sin, 'cause anger without sin will lead to change, but embarrassment only leads to more of the same. When something embarrasses you, you get to feeling like you caused it. And if you think you caused it, you think you can fix it.

A person can't fix nobody else's problems; she can only work on her own. Well, Bernita tried to convince MaBisha that she had things under control. But I don't know what she go and do that for. That only let MaBisha know that she had no control at all.

"Ain't nobody leaving here but him," MaBisha said.

"I'll just wait till she ready to go," Jimmymack told her. He was acting like somebody owed him money and he had come to get it.

"Then you'll be waiting in a police car," MaBisha said.

"Everybody just stop," Bernita said. She wasn't talking nice no more neither. "MaBisha, you can stay but I'll do the talking. Jimmymack, you have to go or I will call the police."

"I just came to give you a ride. Why you gotta act like you shamed of me or something?"

There it was. Here was the real story behind Jimmymack's attitude. He was feeling bad about himself and decided that everybody else felt the same way too. Instead of letting anyone in, he was pushing them away. Bernita had looked beyond his appearance, his job, and his way of talking to see the hurting man behind all that. But just 'cause you in pain, don't mean you get to make everybody else feel it.

Bernita opened the door and stepped out on the porch. MaBisha was right behind her. "Jimmymack," she said real soft. "I've never been ashamed of you. But right now, I don't like the way you're acting. We can talk about this later or not at all. It's up to you."

Too much pride is a terrible thing. Jimmymack made a face that was harder than the one he already had.

"We don't ever have to talk again. Now I see why you were married to a faggot, 'cause you and your dyke were probably doing the same thing he was. I guess you learned it from your man. I don't need you. You need me, you'll see," he said as he stomped off like a tornado leaving town.

Now if you want to hit somebody below the belt, throw something back at them that they told you in confidence and while you at it make sure you take the pain they shared and twist it around to look like it was their fault. Then you got them right where it hurts. It's a good thing Bernita had helped MaBisha through her pain, 'cause now she had somebody to help her through hers.

Well, Bernita went home and did just what I would have told her to do. Turns out she didn't need me to tell her. She wrote a letter to Jimmymack and this time she mailed it.

Dear Jimmymack,

I hope this letter finds you well, and I hope that you will be able to realize the dreams and goals for your life.

I never meant to add sorrow to the pain you already feel. I know that deep down you did not mean the nasty things you said to me. You were feeling rejected. I know that kind of pain. But I also know that when you add insult to injury, the pain does not go away.

I came to you at one of the lowest points in my life. I used you as a stepping-stone out of that pain. For this, I am sorry. Two hurting people can never make a happy union. I understand that more clearly now.

I know that we meet people for a reason, and that it is our job to uncover this reason. You made me feel beautiful, for this I am grateful. I hope that I was able to help you see yourself as I do; wonderful and important.

In friendship,
Bernita Brown

Well, Jimmymack got that letter and his hopes went up. He was thinking that Bernita was apologizing and that they could get back together. But when he called Bernita, she quickly put an end to them thoughts. She tried to explain that she meant that they *could* have been friends, Jimmymack didn't understand.

"Well, can we go out sometime?" He asked.

Bernita said a quick "No," and Jimmymack slammed the phone down and never called back.

CHAPTER 10

writing through the pain

The pen is mightier than the sword.
—EDWARD BULWER-LYTTON

Bernita took that little letter-writing thing and made it into a movement. She saw that whenever she wrote down her feelings, it made her feel a bit more free, so she started going to a class on how to write in a journal. But to each they own.

Bernita would write about everything she did, and what she wanted to do. But what made no sense to me was that sometimes in that class of hers, they would all read what they said was they *private* thoughts. If you ask me, and I know you didn't, some things oughta stay private. There was one man who read about how he hated his mother, and a woman who talked on and on about all the sex she was getting, and how good she was. Now, you know that while I was living I done seen my share of life, but part of the joy in it for me was in keeping it quiet. I guess for some folks the joy is in telling everybody else. They need to brag to feel good, otherwise they won't know if they really did do what they was bragging about. Well, Bernita wrote about her time with Jimmymack and how he made her feel, then she was crazy enough to read it out loud in that class of hers. When she got to the part about how she let Jimmymack go, she made it sound like she was some strong deep soul who finally knew her place in the universe.

Well, that class had a bunch of folks who were looking for their true selves too, so Bernita was in good company. After she read that story about Jimmymack, a woman came up and hugged her.

"I can see that you are on the same journey that I'm on," she said smiling. "My name is Ruth, I would love to introduce you to Truth. It's a movement that will turn you life around three hundred sixty degrees."

Now, when folks come to you with ideas that are just too big to hold on to, don't stand there. Run! Contrary to popular belief, life changes do not happen all at once. True, there are major things that cause big changes, but change happens all the time, step by step, little by little. Besides, if you turn around three hundred sixty degrees, you'd be right back where you started. Anyway, Bernita went to that class, or movement, or church, whatever that Truth thing was and found it to be enlightening, but she needed something more. That was a good thing too, 'cause them folks was all sitting in a room swaying and crying and nobody said a thing. Well, Bernita went on searching for herself. She started going from one weekend self-help retreat to another. They were full of women who were desperate and lonely. They all thought they were bad people. It ain't ever dawn on them that they was just making bad choices. They had the nerve to call them empowerment sessions, but there wasn't no power in them. Now, I know that folks be meaning well, but you know what they say about the road to hell? If you don't, I'll tell you. It's paved with good intentions. I have seen enough from here to know that there are many a good gatherings going on all over the place. There are some people who done got a hold of truth and they been sharing it wherever they go. People like Susan Taylor, and asha bandele, Zora Neale's people, Haki Madhubuti, Rev. Dr. Johnny Ray Youngblood, Rev. Dr. Arlene Churn, Chris Burge, and some others. They can call a gathering like nobody's business and everybody's pleasure. Lord, when they do, people get healed. Not only that, but the ones who are healed get up from their problems and help somebody else with they own. God and all of heaven knows that we need more like them. What we get instead is a bunch of folks who want to be stars. The so-called experts go from one city to the next selling videotapes and books on how everybody can be more like them. But when you look behind the big curtain, you see that it ain't nothing but a show.

Bernita took to going to them living and loving better retreats every chance she could get. She dragged MaBisha to one. That was it for MaBisha. She talked when them experts was talking. She asked all the right questions too, she just asked them at the wrong times. To make things worse, she happened to recognize the leader of one of them break-up, or break-out sessions, whatever you call them.

"I think I know him," she said. The man was teaching people how to breathe on account of he said everybody had forgotten how to.

"Wasn't that man's wife at the shelter when I was a resident?" MaBisha wasn't doing a good job whispering. Bernita tried to get her to be quiet but she was in full swing.

"From what I remember, she had to carry around her own oxygen. I guess he forgot to teach *her* how to breathe."

Well, the director of the camp, retreat, or whatever it was, actually told Bernita that she would only be welcome if she left her friend at home.

"This is a place of learning, and while everyone is valued, we really like to attract only those who are ready to learn." The director told Bernita all of that like she didn't have to pay to be there.

But despite that, Bernita still went in for all of the road to wellness stuff. I really don't have nothing against folks trying to get out of trouble. It just seems like after a while they should have figured that the trouble was wherever they were. You probably thinking that I'm one to talk. After all, I slept my way through life and didn't learn a whole lot for it. You'd be surprised how *not* knowing will teach you what *not* to do. I done told you I don't judge, but that don't mean that I can't talk plain. It's easy to look at the one who went first and talk about what they missed. When I was alive we didn't have all that information you got today. Seems like we didn't have near as many problems neither.

Well, I was telling you about Bernita trying to find herself. She went from one thing to the next. It sure is a lot easier to roll down a hill than it is to climb up one. Bernita was looking all over for herself. Them classes must have gotten her mixed up, because she looked in places she hadn't even been. One week she was trying to go back to her childhood pain. It was crazy. Picture this. Bernita was sitting on the floor, and there was someone sitting behind her with her legs wide open. The woman was supposed to represent Bernita's birth mother. Well, she was hollering just like she was having a baby. There was two other women pulling Bernita by the legs talking 'bout, "Come on out, this time the world is ready for you. You will have love this time."

I was watching that thinking, where's my gun?

Bernita had been writing letters for a while now. They had been helping her to speak her heart and to hear the truth. But when she started in on all that New Age stuff, she was writing most of her letters to herself.

Dear Self,

I am beginning to see things about you that I didn't know before. The real you has been locked away inside the little girl from Sylvania. That little girl had no voice. She walked in the shadows of two very strong women and a ruthless grandfather, but strong doesn't automatically translate to right. You learned to hide your voice and your true self, but now it is time to come out screaming. I will help you. You and I, the grown self, and the child self, will learn to be who we truly are.

With all my love,
Me

Now ain't nobody ever did wrong by looking back. The problem comes in when you don't want to move forward. The next week, Bernita had to get herself regressed. Apparently Bernita's childhood wasn't back far enough, so she had to go back to some other past lives. According to the people who ran that thing, wasn't nobody in Bernita's past that looked anything like her. She was Greek or Chinese and everything else but black. Bernita, bless her soul, was trying to grab hold of all of it. She was needing to find a reason for why she felt the way she did. She was willing to try some of everything. Now, I done told you that God is everything and everything is God. So you know that I know God can use the craziness we invent. My only question is this, why invent stuff when you got enough real stuff to deal with? Bernita was breathing deep and trying to reach what somebody else was telling her about her life as a Chinese emperor. You ever notice these folks are always warriors and kings, or something important? How come they ain't street sweepers or somebody like that?

Seem to me like you shouldn't need to pay somebody to tell you something about you that only *they* can figure out. You get what I'm saying? I don't care if it's a church, a club, or whatever. God don't give somebody else the key and the deed to your house of well-being. It's *your* house and you can come and go as you please. When other people tell you that they got something you need for your life, but only they can tell you how to get it and whether or not you truly have it, you better run in the other direction. Them people don't mean to do nothing but rule over you.

Bernita fell into a lap of rulers. And a ruler that's looking for a kingdom is a dangerous person. Re Member was the name of the man who tried to swallow Bernita's very soul. I ain't lied about nothing else, so why would I lie now? The man actually went to a courthouse and filled out papers to change his name to Re Member. He said he thought about calling himself Member Re, because before you could remember you had to member. That would have been a better move. Anyway, Re Member was a white man who said he was an African/Asian trapped in a white body. He wore African clothes and even spoke Swahili, which didn't make no sense 'cause didn't nobody around him know what he was saying, but that didn't stop old Re, he would just say what he wanted to say in Swahili and then translate to English. *Asante Sana*, that means "thank you." The people who knew Re were on the crazy

side themselves, but he had everybody, including Bernita, convinced that he was sent to them for some kind of special reason.
"You have drawn me into your life for a powerful purpose," he
would say. "It will be your task to discover the reason behind this
attraction." Now, if old Jimmymack thought that Bernita was
ashamed of him, he should have met Re Member. At least Jimmymack had met MaBisha, but Bernita knew that she couldn't show
Re Member around. Ain't it something how, even when you mixed
up in something crazy, you can know enough to keep it to yourself? You think about the times you been around folks who ain't
make no sense. You knew not to take them around the people who
really knew you; the ones who always tell it like it is. I'll give it to
my Bernita, she was hanging out with crazy, but she ain't bring it
too close to home.

Well, when Bernita met Re Member, she met a group of people who called themselves the Enlightened Ones. According to
them, everybody who didn't see things the way they did just wasn't
enlightened. Well, Re Member was one of the Enlightened Ones.
Matter of fact, he was a leader of the Enlightened Ones, which, I
guess, made him a really enlightened one. Re Member took one
look at Bernita and decided that she needed him. He said that she
was his African queen and he would be her African king. I wish I
was making this up, but I don't need to. Life is way more enter-
taining than anything you can make up. Well, Re Member was
laying it on thick, but Bernita was trying to stay focused on her
commitment to celibacy. Oh, yeah, I forgot to tell you, Bernita had
gone to a weekend workshop and learned that all of her problems
stemmed from sex, and that by not having none, she could get rid
of her problems. To each her own. Now, if they had told me that,

they may have had a point, but poor Bernita wasn't getting enough for it to ever be a problem. That would be like saying that the problem with the state of Vermont was that it was overrun with black people. You get my point; if you don't, you should go there and see.

Anyway, Bernita had signed a paper saying that she wouldn't have sex for a year. That wasn't no commitment for her. When I was alive I couldn't have gone past a week. Anyway, Bernita was around the end of her eleventh month when she met Mr. Member. When he told Bernita all that stuff about her being his queen, she smiled and asked him his name. She found him interesting and a little funny in his African clothes. She told herself that he was cute for a white boy, then she went on to convince her own mind to give him a chance because prejudice was not the way of an Enlightened One. When she asked him his name, the man told her Re Member. Bernita thought she must have met him before and that he was trying to get her to remember it.

"I've never met you," she said, trying to be cute and interesting at the same time.

"Re Member," he said again real slow. Bernita decided that he must be telling her to go into herself to remember him from a past life. She wanted to be an Enlightened One, so she thought back on a seminar that taught her how to be herself. Now, how somebody else can teach you to be you is beyond me, but God bless. At that school, or class, or whatever it was, the expert told her that by asking someone else a lot of questions, she would be able to uncover the meaning of her own life. Like I said, God bless. Bernita went to using this method on old Re.

"Who were you to me?" she asked him.

"Re Member," he told her.

"Who are you to me now?" She thought she might get something different, but she got more of the same, "Re Member."

"What have others called you?"

"Re Member."

This went on for some time and he was thinking that Bernita was truly enlightened. She was thinking the same thing about him. And I was thinking, "Who's on first?" It was not until the next session started and a woman named I Am introduced Re Member, that Bernita saw that Re Member was the man's name. She felt like a nut, but before she could see that she was surrounded by nuts, she got caught up in Re Member's presentation. He talked about a journey that takes one back to one's own self, back to the place where we remember and become joined with all that was, is, and will be. Everyone was hanging on to whatever they thought he was saying. All the women were wanting them some Re Member but he had eyes for Bernita, the only one in the room who looked like she was related to an African.

Now there is something to the notion that if somebody wants something, it makes it more attractive to everybody else. I don't know if Bernita would've fallen as hard for Re Member if everybody else hadn't been batting their eyes at him. He wasn't bad to look at, and he wasn't a pretty boy looking for another one, but that didn't make him right for Bernita. Just 'cause somebody ain't the person you just left, it don't mean that they are the one you should be going to. Well, Re Member had a following. I guess you could call them the Re Members. Lord have mercy. When he finished talking they were all standing around hoping that he would make them that much more enlightened. Bernita was way in the back of the room when he held up a single finger to the lips of a woman who was going on about how when he spoke, she felt the power of the moon God.

"Be still," he said, like he was God. When he said it, she acted like he was. He walked past her through the crowd of nuts and pulled Bernita into his arms. "My queen, my love, my sister, my life." Bernita started crying like all of this was real. "I do Re Member." The man actually kneeled down in front of her and kissed her feet. Bernita pulled him up to her and held him close. By now, all of the other enlightened nuts were hugging and crying too.

You ever watch those shows on TV where crazy folks are doing weird stuff like jumping off a bridge with a rubber band around they ankle, or playing in mud with skimpy clothes on? If you have, you may notice something interesting. There is always one black person in the group. Just one and no more. Well, this day, Bernita was the one. I used to wonder where they found that one black person, but now I know it was just one black person that found them.

Bernita found herself at more and more gatherings where she was the only black person. Well, the only black person you could see was black. Re Member and several other people said they were black inside but came to earth in the form of whites so they could understand their oppressors. Now believe me when I tell you that crazy is crazy, no matter what color it come in.

Re Member managed to convince Bernita that her period of celibacy was actually a period of preparation and cleansing for him. "You were cleansing yourself for me." But she never bothered to ask if he had cleansed himself for her. Bernita was so low and desperate that she just jumped right into the madness with him. That night, he took her to a spot in the woods where they were having the retreat and guided her in what he called her rebirth.

But let me tell you how I saw it; he screwed her brains out. I wish I could be more polite, but that's just the truth. Ain't no way you can convince me that she had a brain when she left there. Then Bernita took to following him around like he was really something. People will tell you that Southern folks are slow, and I'm gonna tell you that there's truth in that. We are slow to pick up on things that need to be left right where they is.

Since Bernita didn't have the benefit of a family that passed on common sense, she stayed around Re Member for almost three years. That was amazing all by itself. Nobody that knew her before him knew who he was or what he looked like. MaBisha figured that she was seeing somebody on account of she had that droopy look that comes from loving. She noticed other changes in Bernita too. She started wearing African clothes and saying Swahili phrases. MaBisha figured that she had met an African from Africa and was going to ask her about it, but then she decided not to get too far up in Bernita's business. Bernita still hadn't really got over MaBisha meddling with Jimmymack.

To Bernita's credit, she didn't take Re Member around her work and she didn't talk too much about it to him neither. It was easy to keep things that way since Re Member was always traveling and giving speeches all over the place. She already knew Re Member believed that people chose their own problems in the life they lived before, and if they could only remember why, then they'd be able to rid themselves of their burdens. Re Member had made a movement out of his own name. Bernita was so caught up in Re Member's way of thinking that she hadn't bothered to look at his way of living, but when she did get around to lookin' she didn't like what she saw. As it turned out Re Member had a whole bunch of Memberetts and several baby Res all over the place. The man was an Enlightened One all right, he was an enlightened dog. One day Bernita finally had enough. She wrote Mr. Re Member a letter that should have been a song.

> *Dear Re Member,*
>
> *I hope I can forget you because remembering is just too hard. Zora Neale Hurston wrote that women forget the things they need to remember, but they remember the things that they truly need to forget. I am going to go back to my real roots. I am leaving you to remember the reasons why.*
>
> *Peace and memories,*
> *Bernita*

Bernita had my feisty spirit, but she mixed it with learning and that made me real happy. Sometimes we are so busy trying to give children what we didn't have, we forget to give them what we did. If me or Buster had ever sat down with that girl and told her about our mistakes, she wouldn't have ever had to write a letter to Re Member, 'cause he would not have been anyone that she would have ever known.

Re Member was no more or less than Tyrone or Jimmymack, he just wasn't what she needed. If you go to the beach and all you pick up is trash, don't act like it's 'cause there wasn't no seashells there.

There were all kinds of beautiful men that Bernita could have picked. She wasn't choosing from what was available, she was choosing from her pain.

Life can be either like a car or like a garbage truck. It's up to you. You can take the car on a journey and learn something around every corner, or you can pick up trash at every stop. But you'll take on so much of everybody else's garbage till your own life starts to stink. Now, I know I ain't as smooth as those experts and I ain't deep like old Re, but I know how to tell the truth, and I can spot a problem when it's coming at me. One of the differences between me and Bernita is that when I was alive, I was always honest with myself about myself.

"Babe," I would tell me, "you getting ready for some trouble. You know this man ain't no good," I would say. But hell, he sure do feel good. I always answered myself, 'cause who else can you be that honest with?

There were some real decent men walking around the same places and the same times as Bernita, but Bernita was learning from me long before she even knew she was.

Now, I was watching this, wishing I could just come out and tell Bernita what to do. Even if I did, I don't think she would've heard me. Bernita was too caught up in other stuff to realize that the root of her pain was closer than she had been looking. I know that it wasn't time for me to come all the way into her life yet. The right stuff at the wrong time still ain't right. You got to be in the right season and the right moment to get all that you need. Otherwise, you'll be listening to folks with names like Re Member and How Come. I threw in that last one. But you get my drift. If you fishing for freshwater fish in salty water, you can have a barrel full of fish and still not have what you want. And that ain't nothing but the truth.

on the other side of the world

*Love is like a game of checkers; you got to know
which man to move.*

—MOMS MABLEY

Just 'cause I couldn't actually go to Bernita and tell her how to live her life didn't mean I ain't have no work to do. I looked up and found Ole Ray from Around the Way and we set our hearts in motion again.

When it came to love, things weren't looking no better for Ray's son Douglas than they were for Bernita. Even though Douglas had been writing letters for the kind of woman he wanted to meet, he still fell in with the women who came and introduced themselves to him first. Now women, men only have the confidence we give them, and you know that I know what I'm talking about. Men talk a good game about what turns them on and what they want in a woman, but most of the time they end up with the one who gets them. Next time you out meeting people, you watch and see. The woman who smiles the most and seems like she's easy to approach is the one who will be approached.

Well anyway, Douglas got hooked up with a woman he met when he was delivering packages. She came on real strong and told him how cute he was and how he seemed real nice. She saw him one day when he was delivering something to a business across from hers. She started ordering things just so he would come by. When he did, she was ready for him. On the first delivery, she invited him in for something cold to drink. Douglas said that he was on a tight schedule, but he sure did appreciate the offer. Well, that woman wasn't a bit put off by what would have been a rejection to someone else. She went and got him a cold drink to go and told him that she would take a rain check on their time together. Now she knew that she would see him again, because she was ordering things that had to be delivered by his company. Since she was on his route, she just ordered and waited. One hot day he came in and she handed him a cool bottle of water. Douglas got to thinking that she was real considerate and one thing led to another. Venus—that was her name—asked Douglas out and he went. They went to an art exhibit. Folks who are determined to get what they want know just how to get it. One day, Venus noticed that Douglas had little splatters of paint on his uniform and hands. She figured that he must be a house painter, so she asked him. He mumbled that he was an artist, but didn't say nothing more. Noticing that he was shy and somewhat awkward, Venus didn't bother to push for more information. Later on, she looked up a calendar of art showings and found one that was happening that weekend. The next day when Douglas brought another one of her packages, she told him that she was in a bind and wondered if he could help.

"I have an art show to go to and I really don't want to go alone. I don't know many people who like art, actually I don't have many friends here at all and well, you seem nice and, I promise not to stay too long, but there is a collection that I am dying to see."

She was reeling Douglas in and doing a fine job of it.

"I don't know if you're into this sort of thing, but Dr. Walter Evans has a huge collection of the African-American masters and the opening is tonight. I know it's short notice and all, but I really don't have anyone else to ask . . . "

All of a sudden, Miss Venus let one lonely tear stream down her cheek. Look to me like she was auditioning for the Bette Davis award. Then she dropped her head and turned her back to Douglas, who couldn't help but go to her aid. There are some men who live for a chance to rescue somebody. Why else would we women learn to act helpless? Anyway, Douglas forgot all about his schedule and told old Venus that he would be honored to go to the opening, but slick Venus told him never mind.

"I don't even know you. I'm sorry for bothering you with this. You always seem so nice. I shouldn't have asked you," she said. "It's just that I don't have many friends. I've been divorced for three years and most of my friends were our friends, and well, since he was wealthy and powerful, they chose him over me. I've tried to meet new people, but I have this business to run and I have to work hard and . . . "

Then on cue, Venus let the tears flow. Douglas took her in his arms and held her. He immediately felt for this hard-working, lonely woman who loved the thing that he loved most: art. If she had asked him to dinner or to a dance, Douglas would have said no, but she tapped into the very thing that gave him life. After Venus calmed down, Douglas told her again that he would love to escort her to the opening.

Well, they went to that show and did a whole lot of other things too. Old Venus knew enough to take her time with Douglas and to let him think that he was the one who was running things. She knew that most men thought that they needed to be in charge and so she let them.

Venus had the right name, not 'cause of the goddess of love thing, even though she had lovemaking down pat. No, that Venus was like a flytrap. She would use her beauty and charm to attract a man, just so she could eat him alive. Most times, she turned her attention to wealthy men, but every now and then she liked to do what she called "slumming." She would hook up with an attractive working-class man just so she could make her wealthy man jealous. Now, because I'm seeing life from the other side, I have the opportunity to tell you the whole truth; Venus didn't get that way on her own. She had a mother who told her to marry rich but screw poor. I would try to make it more pretty, but I'm just saying what I learned. Venus wasn't lying when she said that she had been divorced and that her husband's friends stayed by her husband's side. But it didn't have anything to do with his money. Them friends of theirs took his side because they could see just how she was. Venus played around with peoples' lives just to feel good about herself. She would tell one friend that the woman's husband was cheating and then she'd tell the husband the same thing about the wife. To make matters worse, she'd pull another friend into the mess by making them the "cheatee." I made up that word, but you know what I'm talking about. Well, pretty soon everybody was blaming somebody for something. It took a couple of years for them to figure out that all the mess pointed back to Venus. As soon as her husband found out that she was not only stirring up trouble, but that on many occasions she was also the comfort wagon (if you know what I mean) to the husband who thought his wife was cheating, he divorced her as fast as he had married her. (They'd had a quickie marriage in Las Vegas.) Well, Venus was on her own now, but she didn't have to work as hard as she had let on. She had three rather nice divorce settlements from him and the two ex-husbands she'd taken down the same road.

Douglas and Venus were going hot and heavy when he started to notice that whenever they went out, a distinguished-looking man would be present somewhere in the background. The man would sit and stare, but he never approached. Once Douglas asked Venus if she knew who the man was, and she began to cry.

"I was hoping that you wouldn't notice," she told him. "That's my ex-husband. He doesn't want me, but he doesn't want anyone else to have me either."

Douglas was about to approach the man, but Venus begged him not to.

"He's powerful and crazy. He'll hurt you, and make sure that you don't work and that you never make it as an artist," she said.

Venus said that they should just leave the restaurant, so Douglas went to bring the car around. He told Venus that she should come with him. Venus said that her ex would never make a scene in public, he was way too smart for that. She had been standing outside of the restaurant when Douglas left to get Venus's car, but he realized that she had the keys in her purse and went back for them. When Douglas got back inside he got an eyeful. That old Venus was locking lips with the same man that she said was her dangerous and devious ex. When they got done kissing, he handed her a wad of money. He did it on the sly, but Douglas saw it all. The man was just letting go of Venus's behind when she looked up and saw Douglas. And that was the last that she saw of him. Douglas got out of there so quick that you'd of thought the boy was some kind of Olympian. He ran all the way home, tears pouring down his beautiful brown face. He tried to figure out what kind of transaction he had witnessed, but it only gave him more pain. When he got home, he went to the abstract painting he'd been doing of Venus as a surprise. Douglas went to his small but clean kitchen, got a knife, and wanted to slice the painting. He approached the painting with all the rage he'd been feeling, but could not destroy the work. Instead he began to paint over the brown and gold hues. The woman in the painting now had two heads, one beautiful and full of life, the other sad and ugly. The boy took all his anger and put it on that canvas. He was a good painter, and I know his father Ray was proud of him—that he was working his way out of a mess in a good way.

Douglas had some hard days ahead. He didn't make no more deliveries to Venus or anywhere near her place of business, and he never answered her calls. She put up one lie after the other 'bout how he didn't see what he thought he saw, but to that boy's credit, he never gave in. He got out of that mess with Venus, but that didn't mean he was better off. No siree. That boy took to himself like he was the only man in the world that had ever been hurt. He planned to live his life on his own and to love nothing but art. Well, like the old folks say, if you fall off a horse, you got to get right back on, otherwise, you might not want to ride again. Douglas didn't get back on, and the riding thing wasn't gonna be easy. But just like I wouldn't give up on my Bernita, Ray from Around the Way wasn't gonna give up on Douglas either. We might be dead, but we don't ever quit.

Ray got Douglas to write another one of them letters, but it turned into a piece of art. He painted a canvas red and dipped his finger in black ink to write some words, then he did another portrait of Venus. Her head was beautifully painted, but it was attached to the body of a Venus flytrap. The painting read:

> *Beauty in the hands of the enemy*
> *Can only be a trap.*

CHAPTER 12

finding jesus

I found God in myself, and I loved her fiercely.
—NTOZAKE SHANGE

Before I tell you what I'm about to say, let me explain two things. One, Jesus ain't never been lost, and two, God is love.

Okay, I can move on. When Bernita got through with all the rest of her searches, she decided that she needed to find Jesus. Now you see why I made point number one. Let me explain the second. She got hooked up with some people who acted like God was mad at everybody. It's way beyond me why life always seems to swing in extremes.

In all that looking for life, love, and herself, Bernita didn't see that she was letting everybody else tell her who she was and what she could do. I don't fault them men. Sometimes we womenfolk like to look for the problems with the men we pick, all the while forgetting that *we* picked 'em. All of Bernita's men had a reason for doing what they did.

I said that Bernita felt like she had to find Jesus, but let me back up and tell you why. About a year after she got away from her position as the only black person in the room, she had gone back to running in the other direction. Bernita didn't get into none of those blacker-than-black groups though. ('Course, wasn't nobody who thought they were more black than old Re Member.) Anyway, Bernita was at work one day when one of the women at the Passage Way House said she was leaving and going to live with her grandmother. She told Bernita all about her grandma. She was a woman of God and she was full of love.

"Big Mama raised us in the church and taught us right from wrong. It would hurt her heart to know how much I done strayed," she said to Bernita. Well, sometimes folks can miss the whole point of the story but pick up on everything else.

Bernita didn't grow up with the steady love of a grandmother or mother, so when she heard that woman talking she got to feeling that emptiness. Somehow, the feeling got mixed up and she thought she was needing religion. Church was never my hangout. That ain't to say that I didn't keep God in my heart, 'cause I did. And I loved to read the Bible. It was full of wisdom and hope. I read it more than all the good church-going men I knew who loved to point out my sin. They would tell me how I was a sinner and that I needed to go to church and to have God to come into my heart. They usually said all of that right after they zipped up their pants. I felt that God was already in my heart, but I just ain't never found no need for regular church-going. The real truth is that church folks didn't have no need for me. The few times I did try to go, I got talked right up out of there. Now, people will tell you to look at God, not at the people, but the last time I checked it was the people who said they represented God and not the other way around. Don't get no wrong from what I'm trying to get right. There is always some good folks wherever you go, but sometimes we get to thinking that just going to church can make you good.

Bernita was on her way home from work that same day when she found just what she thought she was looking for. Bernita took to her mind that she needed to get to a church and that's what she found. When Bernita was a girl, she did go on her own from time to time. Back then she was walking around with ready-made repetitions; mine and her mama's. People either called her boy crazy or a boy hater. Wasn't none of that had nothing to do with Bernita. She got what we got just 'cause she was ours.

Every one of your ancestors has been through enough that you don't ever have to go through the same stuff again. You see, it says in the Bible that the sins of the fathers and mothers have been passed down to you, but so has their strength. That's what folks forget. If you can just learn to tap into the strength of the ancestors, your life will be much better.

Bernita was on her way home from work when she met up with some people who said they were witnessing for Jesus. Now, you can correct me if I'm wrong, but it seems like to me you would want Jesus to be a witness for you. Well, these folks came up to Bernita the same way Tyrone did. They told her how nice she looked and how she seemed like a good person. When she said thank you, she got hooked.

"Don't thank us, thank God," a woman with a long dress and an even longer face said. "God has given us the power and the grace to meet you. I could tell when I first saw you that God is going to do something special in your life."

Now, you remember what I said about folks telling you something about yourself that you supposedly can't find out without them. Watch out, 'cause somebody is about to tell you something you don't need to hear.

"You lookin' mighty low, maybe you could use a friend to talk to." Now, old Long Face knew not to travel alone. With her was an older woman who looked like the idea that Bernita had in mind for a grandmother. She had a pleasant face. It was the kind that makes you think of baked sugar cookies and homemade rolls. She was round in the body, but not too fat; the very picture of decent, clean living. She wore a small hat and a sweater even though it wasn't too cool. She looked Bernita in the eye and then took her by the hand.

"Honey," she said, "I can tell that you know God, but you have been searching for the love of Jesus."

Now the last I heard, Jesus was the doorway to God. I was wondering how she thought Bernita could have gotten to God, if she hadn't gone through the door first?

Bernita commenced to crying like she hadn't done in a while. The long-faced woman started yelling, "Hallelujah, thank you, Jesus." Then right there on the street corner, she started speaking in tongues like it wasn't nothing to it.

"Helo mo shocka. Ebonta, yeah cordo lo sha."

Now you would think that sitting in heaven, I would have been able to translate. Well, ain't no need to drag out the suspense, I couldn't. Neither could Bernita, because she had no idea that the Holy Spirit was sent to give comfort, not confusion. That woman wasn't speaking tongues no more than I'm talking French. When she got done screaming and shouting, she did a dance, no lie. She asked Bernita if she was saved. Bernita had been through a whole lot of soul searching, but all this was new to her.

"I don't know," she said through her tears.

"Chile, if the Almighty Lord Jesus had come into your heart, you would have known," Miss Oh Happy Day said. By now a small crowd had gathered. Bernita was feeling a bit embarrassed, but she'd done more foolish things than this.

"I want to be saved. I do, but there are so many things I just don't know." Bernita had been feeling so low about herself that everything was sounding right. I'm a tell you something, when you're feeling real low, there are some churches that should be avoided. The hellfire and brimstone places will make you think that you lower than you are, but higher than you'll ever be. Them women were from that kind of church. My Bernita, who hadn't had the love of a real mother, was trying to connect to something bigger than herself.

When them women saw that they had an audience, they really stepped it up. The older lady started singing "Amazing Grace," and somebody that was walking by joined in. They told Bernita to get on her knees and she did. She wasn't alone though. The power of something was moving on that street corner and others knelt down too. They prayed and prayed until they were all crying and rocking. It took the police to break it up. It's a good thing too, 'cause Bernita never got a chance to give them folks her phone number. If it's trouble you're looking for, it's trouble you're going to find.

God had given Bernita strength and wisdom to love life and to share it with others, but she was determined to cast her pearls to swine. She found that someone in the person of Erdell Evan. Pastor Evan was much smoother than the two women from the street corner and he was a whole lot more convincing than all the men she had hooked up with before. Don't get me wrong though, Bernita didn't actually hook up with the pastor.

Trouble runs on a street that's parallel to goodness. It just takes one turn in the wrong direction to get you from one side to the other. Bernita went to work the next day and found a man sitting in the lobby of the Passage Way House. You didn't see too many men in a shelter for battered women, but the ones that did come were usually there looking for work. This man was calm and didn't seem like he was there for work.

"May I help you, sir?" I don't know where Bernita come on her manners; God knows her mama didn't have none.

"Good morning," the man said. "I'm just waiting for Mrs. Ella Staynor. Her mother is a member of our church. She told us about Ella's troubles. We own several apartments and we are going to move Ella into one until she can get on her feet. I'm sorry." The man stood up to introduce himself. "I'm the pastor, Erdell Evan, but everybody calls me Van."

Well, you can probably guess what Bernita was thinking, that this was a sign from God. Here was a pastor with a church and he had a concern for battered women. This was exactly what she was looking for and everything she needed.

"Pleased to meet you, Pastor Evan."

"Call me Van. I feel funny enough being called Mister." Now, Van had a way about him that made you feel right comfortable real quickly.

"When I first became a pastor, my wife, Tricia, made sure that I didn't get no big head. She told the entire congregation to call me Van and that if they ever saw me acting up they should say Pastor Van."

Van sure did make you feel all right about him and about yourself, too. Now, most men won't mention their wife until way down in a conversation. Van was putting her right up front where she was supposed to be. He had learned in seminary school that some women were drawn to preachers just because they were preachers. "Be kind, but not too kind," one of his teachers told him. "You will avoid a lot of temptations that way." Van took all his learning and praying to heart. Or so it seemed.

"This is a very nice facility, Miss—?" Van was looking around but managed to somehow be looking right through Bernita at the same time.

"I'm Bernita Brown. I help run the house."

"Nice to make your acquaintance." Van was all down-home charm mixed with city savvy. "You must have a heavy load on you. Day in and day out, you meet people in their worst of times. Your job makes being a pastor seem like a walk in the park."

"Well, I don't know," Bernita said. "I enjoy helping people in need. Like they say, 'It's a hard job but somebody's gotta do it.'"

"I'm glad the good Lord chose you," Van said. "Thank you for what you've done for Ella and all the women here. The world needs more like you." Van struck the nerve in Bernita that needed to be plucked.

It had been a long time since anyone, other than the residents, had thanked Bernita for what she did. Most men who heard about her work usually got all defensive. They were thinking about the women they had hit, or the ones who had accused them. From what I know, the number of women who falsely accuse a man of abusing them is about the same as the number of people who lie about being mugged. It ain't that many. Still, men have learned from all of them team sports to stick together. Even when they ain't the ones doing wrong, they like to believe that none of their brothers would either.

"Thank you, Pastor Van. I really do appreciate hearing that."

"I told you, it's Van. My wife would take away my dessert if she heard that I had folks putting me on a pedestal."

Van looked like he never touched dessert. He was real tall and lean, but he looked strong just the same. Van wasn't handsome but his smile and charm made you feel happy to be around him. Bernita would've liked to have had a brother like Van. Then she would have told all her girlfriends what a great brother she had and how she hoped to find a man as nice as her brother. You know what the old folks say: "If wishes were horses, everybody would ride."

Ella still hadn't come down so Bernita showed Van the downstairs part of the house. She was surprised by the number of women who knew or recognized Van. They all had something good to say about him. Bernita had lived in this town for going on seven years. She was a bit ashamed that she had never heard of Pastor Van or the work he did.

"Where is your church, Pastor?" She got the up the nerve to ask.

"I'm so glad you brought it up." Van was grinning like a kid with a new toy. "It's actually a learning center. Most folks have been hurt by church and are afraid to go back. I understand though, I've been through it myself." He pulled out a card that was as plain as he was. The words "Wellness Center" were stamped above a twenty-four-hour phone number.

"I've heard of the Center, but I didn't realize that it was a church." Bernita made the mistake of feeling stupid about something she really didn't know about. Folks always confusing ignorance with being stupid. Ignorance is when you don't know; stupidity is when you don't want to.

"We do a lot in our community and all over the city. You should come by sometimes. My wife and I would love to have you."

He was seeming more and more like a brother to Bernita. You know what it feels like when everything is falling into place? It's like when you just did the grocery shopping and you don't need nothing. Or when you get caught up on all of your bills. It's a real good feeling. Only problem is, it never lasts.

CHAPTER 13

biscuit stealers

By the waters of Babylon, we sat down and
wept, and we remembered Zion.

—PSALM 137:1/NEGRO SPIRITUAL

Don't you know Bernita joined that church that wasn't really a church the very first time she went. Everybody kept calling it a "learning center," but how you join a learning center? That I don't know. It sure was different than a regular church though. People got to ask questions and make comments and all.

Van not only answered them, he would ask some questions back. He was funny and smart too. In some ways he reminded Bernita of some of them retreat people. Van made her think of things she hadn't thought of before and he reminded her of the talks she had with herself. The Center had a classroom for children of all ages and a playground and basketball court out back. The apartments Van told her about were right next door. She found out from the question and answer session that a lot of the members were ex-addicts and former inmates, but they mixed well with the college graduates and business people. They was all learning about God alongside one another. Bernita met Van's wife, Tricia, who was as friendly as her husband.

"Hey, Van told me about you and the place where you work. God bless you," Tricia said. She could have passed for Van's twin sister. She was thin like him and real tall too. Bernita wanted to laugh. It wasn't the laughing *at* kind though. It was the laugh that comes up when you happy to see somebody else who's happy.

"Well, Pastor—I mean Van—talked about you nonstop. Ya'll look like the kind of couple that I visualize for the women I meet at the center," Bernita said to Tricia.

"Are you into creative visualization too?" Tricia asked. She was grinning and clapping her hands. Bernita was nodding.

"I love it," Tricia said. "It really relaxes me. But it hasn't been working too well for me lately. I keep trying to visualize myself in a size sixteen, but I'm still in a six."

Ain't it something how folks who are big want to be small, but the ones who are small want to be big? Tricia laughed a laugh that said she wasn't the least bit ashamed of who she was or how she looked.

Tricia invited Bernita to join her family and a few friends for dinner that night. The few friends turned into more like a small class reunion and the dinner was actually a buffet. There were people crammed in every corner of Van and Tricia's house.

Life was looking up for Bernita. She finally felt like she fit in with a group that she needed. But "felt like" and "is" are like the United States and Mexico. They real close, but real different.

The Wellness Center started to take over more and more of Bernita's life. Her friend and secretary, MaBisha, had gone with her a few times, but Bernita couldn't get her to keep going. MaBisha had a history with church-going and it wasn't a good one.

"I grew up in the church and spent most of my life there. I met my no-good husband in church and had to listen to my pastor ask me what I had done to drive him to hurt me. I picked up most of my insecurities in a church, and I am finally learning to like who I am. No, thank you. I've had enough." MaBisha was speaking the feelings of a whole lot of folks.

Bernita didn't let up on MaBisha. She learned from what the Center called "fishing lessons" how to reel in a fish that had a lot of fight. "When you invite people to church, they think of all the congregations and pastors that have caused them pain," Van would say. Reel them in slowly, let them swim around in their own water, then pull them up on the boat. Van taught the fishing class and most of the other classes too. He was in total control, but he made everything at the Center look like everybody had a hand in running things.

Bernita told MaBisha that the Center wasn't like a church at all. It was a place where people came to learn how to really know what the Bible said.

Ain't nothing wrong with change, but when folks get to acting like what's really old is new, get to praying. Bernita did manage to get MaBisha to come to a concert that was at the Center, but she wasn't up front about it. Bernita called MaBisha and invited her to a jazz concert. When they pulled up to the Wellness Center, MaBisha almost didn't get out of the car.

"Let me tell you something about me that you may have missed," MaBisha said. "I don't like being lied to. I didn't like it when I was a child, and I really don't like it now. What really snags my pantyhose is when someone I call a friend tries to trick me into something they already know I don't want to do."

Bernita got to apologizing all over herself. "There really is a jazz concert, it's just being held at the Center. I'm sorry for not telling you. I must have forgot."

MaBisha gave Bernita the same look she used whenever one of the women at the shelter said that her husband had changed. "You know, you're good at a lot of things, Bernita, but lying ain't one of them."

"I'm really sorry. But I love this place and of all the people I know, I would have to call you my closest friend. I would tell you about any other good find, so I would be wrong not to share this one with you," Bernita said.

Bernita's fishing classes were paying off. She was reeling MaBisha in. They went inside and joined about three hundred other folks in what turned out to be a jazzy gospel concert. People were real nice, which was different from the strict church that MaBisha grew up in.

After the concert, Van and his wife came to greet MaBisha.

"I've heard a lot about you," Van told her. "From what Bernita tells me, you are really the boss over at Passage Way."

MaBisha almost blushed. If Van had complimented her looks or anything else about her, MaBisha would have rushed right out of that place. But he knew just which bait went with which fish. MaBisha was proud of the job she did and she was happy to hear that Bernita talked about her to her friends. Van and his wife started out good, but then they went too far.

"If Bernita doesn't treat you right, you can work for us any-time." MaBisha kept right on grinning and laughing, but behind her smile was that radar of hers. Alarms were ringing so loud that she wanted to run. She ain't say nothing though. She had learned from being at Passage Way that she couldn't just come out and tell somebody what they needed to hear. People had to figure out the obvious for themselves. MaBisha didn't know exactly what was wrong, but she trusted her feelings. I would take one MaBisha to any two people with college degrees. Ain't nothing like a hard worker with common sense.

MaBisha went with Bernita to that church that wasn't really a church just one more time. It seemed like Bernita had finally found something that made her happy but it wasn't doing the same for MaBisha. When MaBisha tried to think on why she was feeling so uneasy, she figured that it was because of her own past with the church. She didn't think that was really it, but when she couldn't come up with nothing else, she came to accept the only notion she had.

The more involved Bernita got with that Center, the more she was talking like Van. "I don't have time for anyone who don't make time for God," she would say to the women at the shelter.

Sometimes, we can want something so much that we make believe that we have it, when we really don't. What Bernita really wanted was love and a family. She tried to find love and to make a family with all the men she had been with, and the groups she had joined. Now, she was hearing from the Center that she had been reborn into a family that God had chosen for her. On the top of the vine, the fruit was looking nice and ripe. But if you went down to the roots, you could see all the insects and the rot underneath.

Just like I know that ain't nobody all bad, I can also tell you that ain't nothing all good. Van had done a lot of good, but it turned out that the good he was doing was really to cover up his mess. It's a real shame because God knows Van had started with some good intentions, but that was long before he had became a pastor.

When Van was a child, he dreamt of traveling the world to uncover things, like the man who found King Tut's tomb. He wanted to be an explorer who would find the treasures that black people had left around the world. But one of his mother's friends heard him recite his Easter poem and then decided that God said he was to be a minister. That was it. God spoke to an old black woman about a young black boy, and all dreaming was to stop. Van tried to tell his mother about his dream but she shut him right down, saying, "The devil is sending you visions of glory that will lead to death." Van was about twelve at the time. He was still young enough to dream whatever he wanted. But according to his mother and her friend, God said he was to be a preacher.

You ever wonder why God don't come out and talk to a person directly? Why would God need a middleman? Van didn't have no choice in choosing, so he was brought up as the little preacher boy. Then he became the big preacher boy. He resented church so much hisself that he created the Wellness Center as a way to rebel without completely going against his mother's wishes. Langston Hughes asked the question that we should all be asking: "What happens to a dream deferred?" I sure know. It does dry up like a raisin in the sun. But the problem with a dried-up grape is that it's still good to eat. And desperate folk who want a grape will start to act like they preferred the raisin all along.

Van was doing what looked like good so he could get away with doing things that wasn't nowhere close to right. The more good he did, the more Bernita and all the other folks got to thinking that that they were moving closer to God. All the extra time that Bernita had spent at the women's shelter was now being given to the Wellness Center. Bernita had been a good listener, now she was doing a lot of talking. She told the women at the Passage Way what she thought they needed to hear and didn't bother to listen to what they wanted to say.

"God will help you through this, but you have to give your whole life over to him."

She was saying what she heard Van say, but somehow she had gotten to thinking that they were her ideas. One day, her executive director listened in on a session she had with a new woman. The director didn't want to believe her own ears.

For a long time Bernita had been more than good at helping. She got women to see that they deserved to be happy. Now she was telling them that they were nothing without God. If you tell a broken-down woman that she ain't nothing without God, all she gonna hear is that she ain't nothing.

Well, Bernita's director called her in to discuss the changes that she was going through, but instead of responding in humility, Bernita got all puffed up with pride.

"If I can't share truth with the very people who need it, my time here is over," Bernita said. The woman tried to calm Bernita down. She wanted her to stay. Everyone there did. More than that though, they wanted Bernita to be able to find happiness herself.

Bernita had bought into Van's idea that anyone who was against the Wellness Center was also against God.

She quit her job that day and went to the Center to share what they called a praise report. Van had been hinting for a while that he could really use her on board at the Center.

"Your education and energy are just what I will need here."

When Bernita told Van and Tricia that she had left her job for spiritual reasons, they went to praising God.

"When can you start?" they both wanted to know.

"I'm here, so I can start now."

CHAPTER 14

getting ready

Somebody needs you, Lord, come by here.

—NEGRO SPIRITUAL

Bernita worked even harder at the Wellness Center than she did at Passage Way House. She was there every morning by seven and didn't leave until after 8:00 at night. Her salary wasn't as good as it had been before, but Bernita was thrifty and good with money. She had saved enough to make up any difference. The only problem was that she was giving more and more to the Center. There were so many in need and she had been so blessed. The more she worked the closer she got to Van and Tricia.

Sometimes, if Tricia couldn't make an appointment or go with Van to a dinner engagement, Bernita went along for company. Van would introduce her as his wife's best friend. You can forgive me if you need to, but I think that best friends are for children. It's fine to have someone you confide in more than someone else, but life's problems and joys are too much to dump onto one person. Bernita was going from one event to the next, and Tricia was hardly around anymore. Mark my words and your calendar, if you ask a man about his wife and he get to complaining, you better put your guard up.

One night, Van told Bernita that there was extra work to do. Everyone else had gone home, so Van was free to talk openly. Old Van got to telling Bernita how Tricia never really understood him and how she didn't support his dreams. But when he spoke to the congregation, Center, or whatever it was, he would say just the opposite. Bernita asked him about that.

"I got the impression on Sunday that things had gotten better," she said.

You see, the Sunday before, Van and Tricia were all hugged up. Van had called Tricia to the front and got on his knees to ask her to forgive him.

"I have been neglecting my wife." He was crying and lying like Jimmy Swaggart did on TV. Van told everybody how much he loved his wife. He said that men need to learn when they are wrong and to ask forgiveness. They hugged and cried in front of everybody. Van told the men in the congregation to take a moment to do the same.

"We don't need to pray right now, we need to act." Well, folks were kissing and crying and saying they were sorry. They all meant it too, everybody but Van.

"I am praying that God will heal your and Tricia's relationship," Bernita told him.

"Even God needs a willing partner." This was one of Van's favorite sayings. Usually, he was talking about the need for each person to play their part in their own restoration, but that day he was talking about himself.

"My wife never loved me," he said. "She married me because her family told her that I was gonna be somebody." Bernita didn't know what to say so she decided to say nothing. She had been counseling people for years. Most of the time folk just needed her to listen.

"You ever love somebody who didn't love you?" Van knew the answer. Bernita had confided in him and Tricia about the string of one-sided relationships she had been in. They both told her that God would send her the right man, but that she had to dedicate herself to Him wholeheartedly first.

"I understand," was all Bernita said to Van. She did, but she didn't. She knew firsthand what it felt like, but she didn't see how this could be true for Van and Tricia. They seemed like a perfect match to everyone who knew them.

"Maybe you're just going through a rough time." Well, what did she go and say that for? Van exploded.

"A rough time. You don't know anything," he yelled. "A rough time. We haven't had sex in five years."

I noticed that he didn't say "I," but Bernita was too shocked by all of Van's screaming. Bernita wasn't really hearing what he was saying.

"I have tried to hold my head up and do what God says. But I can't hold on anymore. I have saved hundreds of marriages, but I can't save my own."

Van broke down and started to cry. Bernita didn't know what to do. If he had been one of the women in the shelter, she would have laid a hand on his shoulder or even cried with him.

"I'm so sorry, I didn't know." She was hugging herself and rocking. To Bernita, Van and Tricia had the kind of marriage she hoped to have. Most people who knew them felt the same way.

"Nobody knows what I have to put up with." Now he was rocking back and forth, crying and yelling. "I listen to everybody's problems, but who listens to mine? Where is my help, Lord? When do I get to have joy?"

Bernita started to cry too. She was sad for Van, and for herself. If he and Tricia couldn't make it, what hope did she have? Their love seemed so genuine that she really did pray to God for the same kind of love.

"What do I do for peace, Lord?" Van was screaming and crying. Then he really got to showing out. He threw his Bible in a corner and turned his desk over and slumped to the floor and cried.

"I'm so sorry, Van. It'll be all right." She walked over and put a hand on Van's shoulder. Van held her hand and slowly pulled Bernita down where he was.

"Let's pray for your marriage," Bernita said, pulling back.

Well, what did she go and do that for? Van pushed her and got to hollering again.

"You don't care, nobody does. Just leave. Get out. God hates me. He hates me."

Van started kicking and yelling like a two year old. "Get out, just get out."

Bernita tried to go near him, but he screamed even louder.

"What can I do? Should I call somebody? Deacon Smith, maybe?" Bernita didn't want to leave him alone, but she didn't want to stay either.

"No," Van said. When Bernita got to talking about Deacon Smith, Van was suddenly calm. "I'll be okay. It's just that I have so much to bear. I'm sorry that you had to see me this way."

"Are you sure? I should really call somebody." Bernita started to remember her training.

"No." Van was wiping his face and getting up. "Nobody can help me, nobody but God. I'll clean up this mess and pray."

Men who do dirt with women don't like to be exposed to clean-living men. You look around yourself and you'll see that what I'm saying is true. The Vans of the world always have a bunch of women hanging around. They will say that's because the men are jealous of who they are, and what they have been able to do. The real truth is that they don't want them good men to look them in the eye.

Bernita left. She walked home and prayed the whole way. She was starting to get the same feeling that kids get when they know their parents are getting a divorce. She played conversations over and over in her mind trying to find anything that could have warned her that this would happen. By the time she got home, she was tired. Not tired in body. She was tired in her spirit. For the first time in about a year she wondered if she should have left her job at Passage Way. Don't you know the mind can be a trickster. It will cover up what you don't want to see just 'cause you don't want to see it. The minute you turn your head even a little toward the truth, bingo! You are faced with a bunch of should'ves and would'ves.

Now Bernita didn't know it, but I was looking in places that she couldn't. I could see that old Van didn't spend the rest of the night praying. Well he did, but it wasn't spelled with an "a." He was preying on that same woman that he came to get out of the shelter the day he met Bernita. He and Ella had had a thing going for years and that's how she ended up at the home for women who get beat. When her husband found out about her and their pastor, he went berserk. Sad thing was, he got mad at the wrong person.

That night Ella got the call she was used to getting. "What's up?" Van saved his pretty words for the Wellness Center.

"I was just thinking 'bout you," Ella said. She had been drinking. It was the only comfort she thought she could get.

"Yeah. What were you thinking about?" Van was already driving over to her latest apartment, one he was helping her pay for.

"I was thinking that I probably wouldn't be hearing from you for a while. I mean, you and Tricia are doing good now."

"Shiiiiiit!" Van stretched it out like an old pro. If Bernita had heard him cussing like that she might have fallen right over.

"You know that cow can't stay happy. No matter what I do for her, she acts like it ain't enough."

Ella didn't say nothing about Tricia. She learned a long time ago that with Van things were good one minute and bad the next. He could change with the wind.

"Well, you want me to come over or what?"

This was as nice as Van was going to be. He didn't have to act for Ella. She knew how he really was.

"You know I do." She was pouring another drink. Van wasn't the only actor.

"Good. Go get cleaned up for Daddy."

Ella did just like she was told.

CHAPTER 15

a slice of the
devil's pie

You cannot fool all of the people all of the time.
—ABRAHAM LINCOLN

Ain't it something how you can be away from a friend for a long
time, but then fall right back into step when one of you needs the
other? Thank God for MaBisha. She was still calling Bernita from
time to time just to see how she was doing. Ever since MaBisha
told Bernita that something about the church didn't feel right,
Bernita didn't have a lot to do with her. The night Van had his fit
made Bernita miss her friend something bad.

"Hey, girl, is that you?" MaBisha asked. She had seen Bernita's
name on the caller ID. At first she had the kind of excitement that
you get when you find something that you lost. Then all of a sudden she started to worry. After Bernita left the job at the women's
shelter, MaBisha only got to talk to her friend if she did the calling. She prayed real fast before picking up the phone. "Please
Lord, let my girl be okay."

"This is me," Bernita told MaBisha.

"How you is?" MaBisha laughed. She did a good job of hiding the worry she was feeling.

"I'm doing good. I just hadn't talked to you in a while, and I was making sure you didn't run off with the UPS man." Bernita was doing her best to sound like nothing was wrong.

MaBisha and Bernita used to tease each other about ole UPS. He wore his delivery shorts well. "Somebody's getting a package, but I'd like to open his box," MaBisha said one day.

"Do unto others as you would have them do unto you," Bernita used to say.

After she started going to the Wellness Center, she stopped joking with MaBisha about how good ole UPS looked. Bernita didn't jump up to open the door for UPS like she had done in the past.

MaBisha got up and let the delivery man in and out. When he was gone, she asked Bernita what had gotten into her.

"A little bit of sense. How would you like it if men sat around talking about you like you were an object to be opened?" Bernita was writing and working on something. She didn't bother to look up. I guess she knew best. MaBisha walked over to Bernita's desk and gave her the direct approach she had come to be known for.

"Look, Miss I'm-too-holy-to-have-some-fun, I know that you are my boss, but you are my friend too, and friends should tell each other the truth. I have never judged you even when you needed to be judged. If you no longer want to do what you been doing, just don't. But don't be throwing scriptures at me like I don't know them. Remember, I was reading the Bible back when you were going to all of those self-awareness sessions."

Bernita looked up and responded the way they had taught her

to at the Center. "I didn't mean to appear to be judging. *If* I have offended you in any way, please forgive me," Bernita said. She was doing her "humble yourself" thing. But it wasn't working on MaBisha.

"*If* you offended me? You know you did," MaBisha said. "So, *if* that was an apology, then I accept it. But you don't have to apologize. And to answer your original question, how would I feel if men were talking about me like that? Well, if UPS was one of them, let the games begin."

That night when Bernita asked about UPS on the phone, MaBisha knew that something was wrong.

"Girl, I told you that you were psychic. I went out with UPS last night. His name is Vernon Wilson. He's real sweet. He even asked about you."

Bernita had that smile that comes when you learn that for some people, life just gets better and better.

"You go, girl. You my dog if I don't get a hog," Bernita said. They both laughed. Bernita was never hip. Whenever she used slang, she would add something real lame on purpose.

"Bernita, you sound fine, but I know you ain't. What's wrong?" MaBisha asked.

There are folks who are put into your life to help get you through the worst of times. MaBisha was my personal pick for Bernita. And I must say, I did real good.

"I'm fine. I just wanted to check on you and say hey. We should get together sometime," Bernita said.

Bernita knew that MaBisha wasn't the kind of person to say I told you so. But she wasn't ready to talk about what happened earlier with Van. She didn't even want to hear herself tell that story. Maybe this was just an attack of the devil. It probably was. She knew from life that if you tell somebody about they shortcomings before they got the chance to change, they may never be able to.

The more Bernita thought about it, the more she was convincing herself that everything would be just fine. She promised MaBisha that she would stay in touch and said good night. By the time Bernita read her nightly scripture and prayed for her pastor and his wife, she felt a lot better.

Over across town, Van was feeling pretty good himself.

The next morning when Bernita arrived at work, Van and Tricia were already there. She could hear laughing and joking before she got into the office. She was silently thanking God for answering her prayers. She had no idea that they were laughing about her.

Now, you might be surprised to hear this, but then again, you might not. Folks who specialize in doing dirt also specialize in covering they muddy tracks. Van was telling Tricia that Bernita was needy and jealous. He said she was a good worker, but that if anybody else was around, she couldn't get much of anything done, because she was too worried that somebody else would get all of his time.

"She's always trying to get counseling when she is supposed to be working. We should be charging Bernita instead of paying her."

Whenever Tricia complained that Bernita was hogging too much time, old Van would ask his wife to be patient.

"God is working on her. She will be a tremendous asset to the kingdom when God is through with her," Van said.

Tricia always agreed with her husband even if she didn't want to. She was proud of Van and her marriage. There were times when she felt lonely and unloved. Van could be real moody. But those periods didn't last forever, she always told herself. Besides, Van had a lot of people pulling him in too many directions.

Whenever he came back to himself, Van would shower Tricia with gifts and praise. Whatever temporary pain she felt, was worth it for being married to such a powerful man of God. She told herself years before that she would rather go through hard times than be one of them hard-up divorced women.

When Van got home late the night before, he told Tricia that Bernita had thrown a tantrum because he spent so much time in Sunday service working with the married couples.

"She had the nerve to tell me that I had made all the single people feel bad. When I corrected her, she went to hollering and crying about how lonely she is," Van said.

"You have to deal with too much, honey," Tricia said. "Maybe I should work with Needy Nita from now on."

Van laid his trap beautifully, or so he thought.

"You shouldn't have to be caught up in all of this church mess," Van told Tricia.

"When I married you, it was for better or worse," Tricia said. "A pastor's wife is the second wife. The church is his first. I will help you in any way I can."

Van wasn't the only actor in the family. Tricia had seen the way her husband watched the women. She had even walked in on a few things. But she twisted her mind around to believe that everybody wanted her husband. She told herself that any time he fell into sin, it was because somebody else had trapped him. Tricia was only offering to take Bernita off his hands to make sure her investment was safe.

"Babe, that's probably a good idea. I need to be spending more time with some of the new members," Van said, smiling.

"I'll be glad to help out. We'll see if Bernita throws her tantrums on me. I'll just have to lay hands on her," Tricia said.

They were laughing when Bernita walked in and she took this as a joyful reunion.

"Good morning, this morning. You two sure do sound happy," Bernita said.

"Yes we surely are," Van told her. "And I'm gonna do everything in my power to make sure that we stay that way."

Van grabbed his wife by the waist and held her close. He kissed her long enough for Bernita to turn away. She was proud of her pastor. He was going to work hard to make his marriage work. It looked like Tricia was gonna help. Praise God.

I was watching the whole thing. And I knew that my time to get fully involved was getting closer.

CHAPTER 16

coming into light

What doesn't kill you can only make you stronger.
—SOMEBODY'S MAMA

I wasn't allowed to cross over to Bernita, even though I wanted to. I needed to wait to be recognized by Bernita. You see, what most folks call ghosts is really a spirit memory. That's the memory of those who have gone over to the other side. Y'all usually see us when you need us to help figure out your life. For instance, if you have a problem with drinking, and you had an uncle who drank a lot, you might see him. You gotta think on him first though. That old drunk uncle can hang around for a long time too. He ain't there to scare you, he's there to help. When you get to seeing what you need, you gotta learn to forgive that memory for the cycle they passed on to you. Then we can go on and you can be free.

Bernita was getting closer to remembering her life with me. Only then could she make a connection to the source of her pain.

Bernita worked more with Tricia at the Wellness Center, just like Van had planned. Tricia would watch the way Bernita reacted whenever some people came into the office. She didn't know that Van had lied about them folks too. He had told Bernita that these women were trying to come between him and his wife. But Tricia never figured that Bernita was protecting her and Van's marriage. Why would she? She thought Bernita was her enemy.

Well, Tricia was thinking that her life was perfect as it was. She knew it wasn't gonna get no better. But she had one of them vested interests in making sure that she believed her lies and Van's. People can do wrong by themselves and for themselves, but they need help to keep it up. Folks like Tricia are not victims. No sir, no ma'am. Those are the ones who hold the stones for the stone throwers. If the Tricias of the world didn't find the stones, then the Vans of the world couldn't keep throwing them. One just as bad as the other, 'cause neither would act out on they own. Tricia pretended to be Bernita's friend. All the while she and her husband were playing her for a fool.

They got to telling others a bunch of mess about Bernita too. When no one was looking, Van would call Bernita from his phone and then hang up. She would see that he called, so she returned the favor. When she did, he went to showing everybody his caller ID.

"Here she is again. What does she want now?" Van would ask.

Everybody at the center started looking at her funny. To make matters worse, Van was telling Bernita about everybody else's financial needs.

"Sister Brown needs this," Van would say. "Brother Blue needs that. We're having a hard time meeting the needs of the people."

Van and Tricia never came out and asked for nothing. Oh no. Matter of fact, old Van made a point to play down offerings.

"You all should only give what you can afford," He told the members. "You should pay your bills first, and then give to God." Ole Van sure had everybody hoodwinked. That's what he said in front of the congregation. But one on one was something else. Privately, he would tell folks how nobody was giving and how he and his wife were way behind in their bills. Well, everybody saw, or thought they did, how hard he worked. They knew, or thought they knew, that he was a man of God.

Bernita was one of the individuals he picked for his private signifying sessions. She had a good chunk of money put away and she had money sense for making more. Van picked her brain and her pocketbook. It's a terrible thing to have somebody use you, but it cuts to the core when they try to take all you got and make you feel like it ain't nothing. That's just what Van did to folks. People would give all they had and he would tell them to they face, "I would say thank you, but it's not for me, it's for God. Besides, we owe so much that this is only a drop in the bucket." The saddest members would go off and ask God to help them get more.

God don't cause mess, but God sure will allow us to go through the things we accept. The joy of it is that eventually God will use it toward our good.

Bernita was dipping into her savings so much that after a bit she wasn't dipping, she was swimming, and all of it was going to the Wellness Center. The only ones who seemed to get any better were Van and Tricia. By this time, Bernita was making the same mistake she had made in past relationships. She was doing all kinds of justifying and told herself that it was worth it. Only now, it wasn't Tyrone, Jimmymack, or Re who was the focus. This time it was the Center.

Whenever folks use God to back up they mess, it can really put you in a bind. If Bernita ever got to feeling like something wasn't right, she could tell herself that she was doing it for the Lord.

One time she mentioned to her new best friend Tricia that she was worried about her own finances. "I do so much but I seem to be getting so little back," Bernita said.

"What does the Word say?" Tricia asked her.

"'Do not grow weary in doing good, for in due time you shall reap your reward,'" Bernita responded.

"In due time, sister. Just be patient and wait on the Lord." Tricia said something right, but she was using it for wrong.

More and more money was going out of the members' savings accounts and into the Wellness Foundation. That Foundation wasn't nobody but old Van and Tricia.

Bernita was more stressed every day. Now, I know y'all like to say that you are too blessed to be stressed, but let me just tell you something. Stress don't lie. It's God and the body's way of telling you that something is off balance. Instead of ignoring it, you need to listen closely. Bernita wasn't listening at all. She worked harder. After all, this time she wasn't trying to impress a man. She thought she was doing it for the Lord.

Bernita had been at the Center for more than a couple of years when she missed her first day of work there. She had a fever and was sweating something bad. When the mind keeps putting the body in harm's way, the body will protest. It won't be none of them "We shall overcome," peaceful kind of protests neither. It's gonna be one of them drum-beating, in-your-face kind. That's what was going on in Bernita's body. She called in to tell Tricia that she wasn't feeling well, but Van answered. When Bernita told him that she would be staying home, Van got to breathing heavy.

"I'm gonna come over and pray with you," he told her.

It's a shame that folks who do wrong can spot a window of opportunity better than the ones who do good.

Van got to Bernita's so quick you would have thought that she said she had some money for him. This time it wasn't money he was after. Bernita opened the door and Van could see how sick she really was. The child was pale and all worn out.

"It's probably the flu. I don't know if you should come too close," Bernita said.

Van said he wasn't scared of no flu, that he brought his anointing oil with him. When he told Bernita how bad she looked, he didn't have to lie. The child was really sick.

"I'm going to have to do a special anointing," Van told Bernita.

He pulled out his oil and started to pray. He got up and walked back and forth in her apartment while he talked to God. At least, that's who he *said* he was talking to. Bernita was coughing and sneezing so much that even I wanted to leave, but since I didn't have a physical body to worry about, it didn't matter. When Van got through walking and talking, he put his hand on Bernita's forehead. He put oil on it. Then he touched her neck and moved down to her shoulders. He touched her back and then laid hands on her stomach. Then he got on his knees and laid hands on her feet. He poured oil on them and started rubbing. Bernita was dizzy but she wasn't dumb. She stepped back and almost fell. Van was quick. He jumped up and grabbed her by the waist.

"You are very sick and you may die. I need to do a deeper anointing," Van said.

"No, I'm feeling better," Bernita said. "You should go. I wouldn't want you to get sick too."

She was talking, but Van wasn't listening. You see, when folks like Van make up they minds to do something, they can't see a way to stop. He pushed Bernita down on the couch and was trying to open her robe.

"I need to do a special anointing." He was talking and pulling, but Bernita held her robe closed.

"I'm fine, Pastor," Bernita said as hard as she could. From the day Bernita first met Van she had been calling him Van. Now, she called him by his title. She was hoping that it would help him to see more clear. When women get hemmed up like Bernita did, the first thing they do is blame themselves. They somehow get it in they head that what they see ain't real, and that they caused it.

"I was just praying for you, Bernita. Why would you think that this is something dirty?"

Van got up and started to go. But he wasn't going to go easy.

"Do you want God to help you or don't you?"

"I do, but I don't think—"

"Bernita, how many times have I said God is not interested in what we think? God wants us to submit ourselves to his will," Van said.

Bernita tried to measure what Van was saying against what she knew was right.

"Open your robe and let me pray for you." Van was stern this time. "Obedience is better than sacrifice."

Van was almost yelling. Bernita didn't open her robe, but he started touching her anyway.

Bernita was feeling lower than she ever did. Something in Bernita's head took her back over her life. She saw her failed relationships and the pain of her childhood. She remembered the beating me and her mama put on her, and she saw her granddaddy calling her a wench. She looked back on the place where she slept as a child and she looked up and saw me. I was there on that twin bed with a man. There had been many, but Bernita remembered this one in particular. It was Reverand Simms. He was touching me the way Van was touching her. She looked at me and I looked right back.

It scared her, but it also gave her the strength she needed. She jumped up and screamed, "No, no, no, no, no, you will not do this to me."

Van looked at her like she was the crazy one. Then all of a sudden, he started to cry.

"I am so sorry. Please, please forgive me," he pleaded. "I have never been unfaithful. The devil, the devil, he was using me to destroy our friendship and all the work that God is using you to do. Please forgive me. I don't . . . this has never happened."

He was trying everything he had in his trunk.

"I guess I have always had feelings for you, Bernita." Van went into his crying routine. "I have never acted on my feelings. God has helped me to stay on track. But you have always been so nice. Whenever we are together we accomplish more than I can alone. Lord knows I've tried. You are so beautiful," he said.

Van was telling Bernita everything a woman was supposed to want to hear. Only problem was, he wasn't the one she wanted to hear it from.

"I need you to forgive me. You gotta know that this is not who I am," Van said.

Bernita was moving away and trying to talk but she couldn't come up with the words.

"I really do love you, Bernita, but I refuse to break my marriage vows," Van said.

He was acting like somebody had asked him to break his vows.

"Please understand," Van said to Bernita.

She stood up and moved over to the door. She opened it, and Van left.

CHAPTER 17

out of darkness into the marvelous light

You have turned the place of worship into a den of thieves.

—JESUS OF NAZARETH

Bernita stayed home the whole week. She got over the flu, but there was more ailing her than a virus. Her absence gave Van plenty of time to spread a blanket of lies.

"Tricia, you were so right," Van said. He walked into the office looking like he had been attacked.

"What about?" she asked. Tricia loved when Van admitted that she was right. If a man as powerful as he was being taught by her, well, she must be *somebody.*

"Look at the caller ID, baby," Van said. Tricia looked at a bunch of calls and saw Bernita's home number.

"She called here this morning crying," Van said. "Bernita said she was gonna kill herself. Well, I rushed over there and she was in this Victoria's Secret thing."

Tricia stood up, about to say something, but Van stopped her. He needed to get his lie told.

"She had an empty bottle in her hand and she was acting all funny. I was trying to get her to tell me what she took. The next thing I know, she was all over me. I told her I was leaving and she started saying, 'No, no, you will not do this to me.'" Van said, shaking his head.

Bernita *had* said those very words, but you already know why she was saying them. To a point, so did Tricia. She had heard enough of Van's "this-woman-is-after-me" stories to see a pattern. But Tricia didn't want to admit that to anybody, and she surely would not admit it to herself.

"I'm going over there," Tricia said. She was up and on her way. "I'm tired of these women coming in here trying to destroy the ministry."

Now, Tricia knew enough to defend the church instead of her marriage. Both were a sham, but she had a better case for the church.

"Calm down, Tricia. I handled it," Van said. He was looking tough and holy at the same time.

"Did she take any pills or was it another one of her needy cries for help?" Tricia asked.

Van was looking just like he had been through something he didn't cause.

"She didn't take anything," He told her. "I had to force the truth out of her. She finally said that she was trying to get me over there. She said she knew I loved you too much to ever want anybody else, but she needed me too."

"Van, you poor thing," Tricia said. She walked back to Van and put her arms around him and continued, "This is the very thing that brings down so many ministries. The devil uses these lonely women to try to put an end to God's work. When will your suffering end?"

Van hugged his wife.

"I'm so tired. But if this is what it takes to destroy the strongholds of the enemy, then I will stand. I'm just glad that I have you. The next time you warn me about somebody, I'm going to listen."

Van took his wife to lunch and the mall and bought *her* something from Victoria's Secret. He said that Tricia was the only woman he ever wanted to see dressed like that.

Van repeated his story to a couple who were in what he called his "inner circle." He told them that he needed someone else to know in the event Bernita tried to pull anything. Van's a sneaky Pete and I'll tell you true, he didn't have to tell another soul, because that couple told everybody they knew and Van knew they would.

When nobody called on Bernita the entire time she was out, she knew something was wrong. The Wellness Center took pride in visiting folks who were sick and shut in. She had done a lot of those visits herself. Bernita had been a friend and help to a mess of folks. Surely one of them could've returned a favor. But by now, as far as the church was concerned, Bernita was one of them untouchables. Even Mother Teresa couldn't have helped.

Bernita's only fault in all of this mess was that she didn't leave the Center when the door was open. She did like most people do. She stayed there long enough to get that same door slammed in her face.

That week her body was getting better, but that was all. Dur-

ing that time she convinced herself that what Van said was true, all
this was just the devil testing them and trying to destroy the work
of the ministry. She prayed and fasted to be able to hear the Word
and ignore her doubts. That Sunday, she got herself together and
went back to the Wellness Center. Before she even got inside, she
was getting all the stares and whispers that Van had conjured up.

"Good morning, Brother Ray," Bernita said to one of the ush-
ers. "Nice to see you."

Brother Ray was one of those men that was always happy.
When he first came to the Center, he had just gotten out of a
halfway house where he had been recovering from crack addiction.
He had been clean for three years. His wife had taken him back
and so had his old employer.

"Always a good day when you in God," Brother Ray would always say. He felt that the Wellness Center had saved his life. It
never crossed his mind that the God light that was in him and the
prayers his grandmother had sent down from up here came together and set him free.

This morning, Ray wasn't looking happy. When he saw Bernita
he ran over to his wife. She held on to him like Bernita was a kid-
napper and her husband was a kid. Bernita told herself that she
was imagining things. People who are good don't go looking for
nothing else. That's why they get trapped. It's only folks with bad
intentions who can see them in somebody else.

She sat in that service, Center, whatever it was, and listened as
Van got up there and preached about how the devil was busy. He
talked on and on about how there was a Judas in the midst, but
that even Judas had a purpose. When he got near the end, he
started his crying thing.

"Someone here is going to betray me," he said.

It didn't take a soothsayer to know that he was talking about Bernita.

"The ministry is under attack, but we will stand," Van hollered. "We will stand."

He called everybody up to pray. When it was Bernita's turn, he called Tricia over. He had her lay hands on Bernita instead.

The situation was dark, but Bernita wasn't blind. The light of truth came on and she could see. It says in them gnostic Gospels that when a blind man and a sighted man are in darkness, both are blind. But when the light comes, the sighted man can see. Bernita got up from that altar where they were laying hands on her and then left. To her credit, she never looked back.

Bernita spent a couple of weeks of agony alone. She had given herself to the Wellness Center for years and not one of them folks bothered to check on her. From where I sit I could see that one day a woman from the Center brought Bernita's name up in a Women's Fellowship group. The women had been talking about winning souls for God and bringing the stray back into the fold.

"She's a stray," Tricia said. "A stray cat. You know what cats do when you try to rescue them? They'll scratch your eyes out."

That other woman didn't say nothing else.

Them weeks at home were good for Bernita, but the time was hard on her too. She had the time to think through all that had happened, and that gave her the strength and dignity to get herself together.

Part of the reason Bernita stayed home was that she was afraid of running into anyone from the Center. The other reason was that she was feeling real low. She wondered and worried how *she* had gotten herself into this mess. Now, if you ask me, the enemy's real weapon is in making us blame ourselves for someone else's guilt.

Before going to church, Bernita had been to every self-esteem—raising workshop that came her way. They kept saying you gotta love yourself, you gotta tell yourself that you're worthy. What they didn't ever get around to was this: Self esteem is for the self, but that ain't where all of it comes from. It comes from the people around you. If you around people who tell you that you dirty, then that's just how you'll feel. If they show you love, you will learn to feel worthy of it.

"That you?" MaBisha said into the phone, recognizing Bernita's phone number on her caller ID. All Bernita could do was cry. But that's all that was needed. Don't you know that your groaning speaks louder than a beautiful prayer? MaBisha said, "I'm on my way."

Everybody needs a MaBisha Moore in they life. She the kind of friend who don't ask what happened. She don't even ask if she can help. She just up and help.

CHAPTER 18

good and ready

Like a bridge over troubled water.

—SIMON AND GARFUNKEL

Now, some people don't like to hear folks say that they been lucky. They say, "The luck is in the Lord and the Devil is in the people." Them people will say, "I ain't lucky, I'm blessed." Most of them is lucky. Blessed is when good stuff happens to good people, luck is when good stuff just happens. But there's more to it than that. To truly be blessed is to know that God is enough. Most folks run around yelling, "I'm blessed" whenever somebody ask them how they doing. The whole time they saying it they trying to get God to give them more stuff.

But Bernita *was* blessed. She wasn't content with who she was, but she was happy with what she had. She was lucky too. Goodness followed her even when she was walking around in a whole heap of bad.

When MaBisha got to her house, Bernita could barely talk.

MaBisha made tea and waited till Bernita could speak. When Bernita got started, it was like she wasn't going to stop.

"I wish I could've listened to you. I feel so stupid." Bernita was low, but telling her story out loud was helping her to get better.

"I ought to go over there and kick some ass," MaBisha said. She would have done it too.

"Ain't no need for you to get into trouble," Bernita told her. "I don't feel like visiting prison just to have somebody to talk to."

"You right, but I got a cousin who will do it, turn himself in, and do the time, all for twenty dollars and a Big Mac," MaBisha said.

Bernita laughed a real laugh for the first time in too long. She and MaBisha stayed up all night. They talked, laughed, ate, and talked some more. MaBisha gave Bernita the update on her and Vernon, the UPS man.

Now you already know that Ray's son drove a delivery truck, and you know that there is no such thing as a coincidence. All I'm going to tell you right now is, God sure is good.

Things were hot and heavy with MaBisha and her new man Vernon. Bernita and MaBisha talked about the shelter and how not much had changed. There was one huge difference though— the director was gone and they were in search of another. MaBisha said she knew just the person for the position.

It didn't take long for Bernita to bounce back. The next day she filled out the paperwork they needed. The folks at the shelter got Bernita started the very next week.

Bernita's life was back on track. From time to time she would run into the Wellness Center folks, but none of them had anything to say to her. To make good even better, Bernita went back to writing them letters again. She was learning to take the good from all the stuff she learned and live.

Dear Self,

I am writing you this letter to let you know that you will be just fine. Love will come your way when the time is right and you are right for the time. You have been through a great deal, kiddo, but you are strong, you are beautiful, and most of all, you are here. Stay strong, on track, and in peace.

Somewhere out there, someone is being prepared to love you.

Signed, Me

P.S.

I love you now.

Dear God,

I know that You are with me. You gave me the strength and power to create and I put it into a church. We are told to go into all of the world and preach the gospel, but I got caught up in the Center. I left one bad relationship and found another. The Center was not the relationship I needed nor could it have been. I needed a relationship with You, not with a place or a person. In a way, I was also using Van. In him, I tried to have the brother, father, and family that I never had. I made the Center my refuge, but you are my refuge. The dysfunctional relationship I had with the church was not a one-sided thing. I share in the responsibility for my pain. Thanks for helping me to get out and go on.

I will always need You and be with You. I no longer need to be told how to find You. I will do that on my own, with Your help.

Thank you God.

After I read that letter I knew that in time, Bernita was going to be just fine. Things were just getting back to normal in her life when Ella, the woman who caused her to meet Van in the first place, was back at the shelter. She had been beaten up real bad. It was much worse than the first time. Ella told the Passage Way counselor she didn't have noplace else to go. When Bernita saw her name on the log, she prayed first and then went in to see her. Both of Ella's eyes were swollen shut and her lip was big and blue. She still had bruises around her neck. There were bandages on her wrist and a cast on her leg. Bernita found out that day that no matter how low you've been, there's always somebody who's been lower.

Ella told a story that would have made a gorilla go bald. She started from the beginning and talked about how Van had been the cause of her coming there the first time. She had been a member of his clique when he'd first started out. Ella said that they had a thing going for as long as he had been married to Tricia. Van had been telling Ella that she had caused him to sin.

"I was pure before I met you," he told her. Ella believed him and let herself get roped into years of abuse, but she didn't do it by herself. You can't have a victim without an abuser.

Van started the whole thing just like he tried to do with Bernita. Ella had had the chance to walk away like Bernita but for some reason she didn't have the strength. Sometimes people get so roped into mess that they start to thinking that's all they deserve. That's what happened with Ella. Every time she got a little strength to get up, Van handed her another lie. First time, he led her to believe that he was gonna leave Tricia. Second time, he told her he was gonna leave the Center and the town they were in and they were gonna go somewhere and start new. The third time he didn't need to tell her anything. By then she started believing that her life was meant to be miserable.

"You are my thorn in the flesh and I am yours," Van told Ella one night. He was getting up off of her when he said it. Ella was sure that one of her children was his. Bernita was the first person she ever told.

"Why didn't you ever tell anyone?" Bernita asked her.

"Why didn't you?" Ella didn't know what happened with Bernita and Van, but she knew something went down. Two months before, Ella had asked Van where Bernita was. She said she hadn't seen or heard from Bernita. Van went to screaming about how Bernita had tried to run the Center and his life. Ella never asked again.

Ella saw Bernita's escape as a way out for herself. She went to needing less and less from Van and took to not answering the phone when he called. If he came to her apartment, she wouldn't open the door. By then, Ella had gotten a job and was finally able to pay her own bills. Ella didn't need Van, but he sure did need her. What most people don't realize is that folks like Van really can't stand to be alone. They need someone to torture, or they feel tortured themselves.

Van would leave messages on Ella's phone machine telling her that he would have her evicted. After all, he helped to get her the apartment in the first place. Eventually he made good on his threats. Ella moved in with a female co-worker and found love with her beautiful friend. It was the first time that she felt whole. But when Van got wind that she was shacking up with a woman, he hit the roof, and Ella. Pride wouldn't allow Van to have something he thought he owned to be taken by anyone else, especially another woman. One night he snatched Ella into a car and drove to a dark alley and beat her badly. Had it not been for a man most people would have called a bum, Ella might've still been lying there. The man went to a liquor store and called the police. Then he went back and waited until they arrived.

When the police asked Ella if she knew who attacked her, she said she was jumped from behind. The police figured that Ella was lying, but couldn't force her to tell the truth. When she was released from the hospital, Ella called the shelter and MaBisha went and picked her up.

"You got to tell the police," Bernita told Ella.

"No, I don't," Ella said. "Van said he would hurt my children. One of the men from the Wellness Center called my girlfriend and told her that we better leave the pastor alone. That man don't know what really happened, and even if he did, he wouldn't believe it."

Ella hit that nail right on the head. It wasn't that folks couldn't believe something so bad, they just didn't want to. You ever notice when women or men tell on somebody who supposed to be important, everybody starts questioning them. Bernita knew from her own life that Ella was right. Van and Tricia had done enough good for folks to think they couldn't ever do bad. Bernita told Ella her story so neither one of them had to feel alone. Remember I said that when a story of pain is told out loud, folks get set free? Well, this was one of them times. People who been brought down by life get to thinkin' that talking will make it worse. It's the *not* talking that adds the salt. We think nobody will believe us, or worse still, that we will get the blame. But the saddest thing is when we think we ain't got nobody to tell.

That's what happened with me when I was alive. I never looked around to find anybody to talk to. So I kept livin' the way I learned. After a while, wasn't nothing could be done that I hadn't done to myself. If you've got a sad story to tell, say it to somebody who will help you. If you ain't got nobody like that living, then tell it to the dead. Just talk to them, and you will be heard.

CHAPTER 19

coming out of the cold

I was reborn when I was broken.
—MAXWELL

Ella stayed at the shelter until she got better. Then she and her girlfriend and kids packed up and moved out of town. She wrote to Bernita from time to time to say how things were going. Her life was getting better one day at a time. A pain like hers takes a long time to heal, but it does heal.

Bernita didn't want to let Van just keep living like nothing happened. She wanted to take action. Not for revenge though. Bernita wanted to make sure he didn't ruin no more lives. The Bible says that when you return evil for good, then evil will never leave your house. Van got his. After Bernita left the Center others started to do the same. The light she brought with her was gone. All the things that she did to make the Wellness Center better, stopped after she left.

When nasty people get desperate, they can't help but act

worse. Van was losing his power of influence and it was driving him even crazier than he already was. The tantrum he threw at Bernita's wasn't nothing in comparison to what he did after she left. More folks started feeling that something wasn't right and were getting up out of there, so there was fewer and fewer of them for Van to hide behind.

He's down to about six people now. They lost the Wellness Center building, so they meet in the apartment he and Tricia live in, the same one he took Ella to when he first got her from the shelter. That old saying is true: What goes around really do come back around. If what you sent around is stank, then it's gonna be right funky when it gets back to you.

Bernita left the pain and shame of the Wellness Center behind, but she crawled into a shell. She still went to work and functioned like the professional she was. But she wasn't taking no more chances with her feelings. If it hadn't been for MaBisha and her job, Bernita might not have mattered to anybody living.

By now you may be wondering what was going on with my man Ray and his son, Douglas. Well, after the hurting Douglas got from Venus the Flytrap, he poured his whole heart into painting. He still drove the delivery truck though, bless his soul. His art-work was selling in top galleries all over the place. He was making more money than even the top man who ran the delivery company, but driving gave him the chance to do something normal. It was what Ray called his "window to the world."

After that mess with Venus, Douglas changed his route and started driving in a completely different area. This time, he wasn't in the classy business area. No siree, he chose to work in the neigh-borhoods that most drivers wouldn't go to. There was only one other driver besides him who actually requested that route. That driver became Douglas's friend and brother. If you been paying attention then you already know that Douglas been hanging out with Vernon. That's right, the same good-looking, tight-shorts-wearing driver that MaBisha had hooked up with. Life sure do know how to wrap itself back to where it need to be.

CHAPTER **20**

life is not the beginning

*I looked over Jordan and what did I see? A band
of angels coming after me.*

—NEGRO SPIRITUAL

Bernita had just left college and moved up North when I met my
Maker. She'd left Sylvania after high school and didn't look back.
Bernita never called none of her family and we never tried to find
her. Sadness sure do beget more sadness. Well, I told you I married into the name Wright, but I ain't tell you anything more about
my husband. Charlie Wright was his name. Everybody called him
Goody on account of he was so good. For me, there was never a
more decent man that walked the earth. I ain't including Jesus
'cause that just ain't fair. Goody grew up in Sylvania, and even
though I didn't remember him, we went to school together. He sat
behind me in eleventh grade. I didn't know it then, but Goody had
a crush on me. He told me later that I always looked like I needed
a friend. There are some men who are attracted to a woman's sadness. Seem like they were sent here just to take care of somebody.

When Goody left the Navy he lived all over the world. He got married, divorced, remarried, and widowed. He came back home when his second wife died. We ran into each other one night down at Tubby's Bar. Goody remembered me right away. He had been all over the world, while I had stayed right in my little town. I had been through more men than I could count. I didn't remember the ones I had slept with, and I surely couldn't remember somebody just 'cause they sat behind me in school.

That particular evening Goody came over and gave me a big old hug.

"You remember me?" he asked.

He was grinning up a storm. That storm sent a bolt of lightening down into my heart and I got to smiling back.

"Should I remember you?" I asked back.

I was already a little tipsy and Goody was making me dizzy. He told me who he was and how he knew me. Then he reminded me of a day in high school when a girl beat me up for sleeping with a boy she liked. Goody said he wanted to help me, but the other kids wanted to see a fight so they held him back.

"I wish you had helped," I told him.

I showed him the scar I still had over my right eye from when that girl cut me with a broken bottle. I told Goody that my sister Buster got that girl back later after I lost that fight. That was the only thing I can remember her ever doing for me. I don't need to tell you 'bout how sad it is for somebody to show love by showing hate.

Well, me and Goody talked all night. I asked him if he wanted to go to my place but he said no. I was feeling a little bad and figuring that he was too good for me. I was 'bout to leave when Goody asked if he could see me again the next night. I was confused, but I told him yeah just the same. I hadn't ever seen nobody two nights in a row if I hadn't done something with them on the first night. Well, Goody came around every night for a month and he ain't try nothing. I did though. I was thinking he didn't like me 'cause that's the only kind of like I ever knew. Goody told me that he loved me and wanted to make sure that I felt the same way. I said I did right then. He laughed, kissed me on the forehead, and went on home.

At the end of that month, we got married. He went and bought us a little house over in Dublin. I figured we was moving out of town because he was a bit shamed of me and I told him so. Goody laughed his laugh and said that I was shamed of myself.

"Ain't no shame in my love for you, woman. I just want you to be able to live without everybody saying something hurtful."

Now Dublin wasn't that far away, only about eighty miles, but that was enough for a new life. Mudslingers don't like to work too hard.

Me and Goody had it nice. He was retired and I was just tired. We fished and took long country rides like we had been together for years. Goody took me to movies and to hear all kinds of music. It don't take much to make a miserable person happy, but Goody heaped kindness on me like my birthday came every day. We had it like that for three years.

Now you can look on what happened later in one of two ways. You can either think stuff ended before it had a chance to get comfortable, or that God gave me some comfort before stuff ended. I pick door number two.

One day me and Goody drove over to Sylvania to put flowers on his and my mama's graves. I had never done it before but Goody said I should. He'd been showing me a whole lot of love and I was starting to learn how to give some back. We had a little picnic in that cemetery like we had been doing it forever. Something 'bout spending time in that cemetery made me think of Bernita. I told Goody about her and how I was ashamed of how I treated her. I cried and so did he. Then he got a look that I couldn't figure. He looked real sad, but kind of happy too. I asked him what was going on, and he said that everything had a season.

"When the time is right, you gonna get just what's right," he said.

I didn't know what he was talking about, but his smile made me feel that everything was okay. Goody said he could try to find Bernita on that internet thing and that made me feel real glad. Most of my sisters had moved away and them that didn't wouldn't speak to me anyway. It was gonna be good to be in touch with some family after so long. God sure is wonderful. It was starting to smell like rain, so we packed up our things to get home.

When we left to make our way back, I had to stop to use the facilities. I came out from the bathroom and saw the prettiest sky I ever did see. It looked like the clouds had opened up to let the sun shine right down on me right in the middle of a sky dark with rain clouds. Those clouds were as round as a pregnant woman who was way overdue. In the center of them clouds was the sun in all her glory.

She was shining for me.

I was staring up into the sun and didn't hear Goody calling my name. Just when I turned to tell him to look at the sky, a drunk driver hit me dead on. I know that's a poor choice of words, but when you dead, you just say it like it is. The car was moving too fast for me to feel a thing. But that sure was a nice day.

Goody almost died with me. He and Tubby, the owner of the

bar where we met, were the only folks who came to my funeral. I was glad to see that in the end, I had two folks who really cared. If I had gone any sooner, there might not have been none. Goody stayed to himself for some time and it's only now that he's got some life back. He was living in a shell just like Bernita. One day I whispered Bernita's name in Goody's ear, and he came right back to who he was and what he needed to do. He got up, and got on that internet thing to look for Bernita. He found my niece right off. Somebody had written something real nice about her and the work she had been doing. It sure is a good thing to be able to leave tracks that ain't muddy.

I had been missing that child most of my life and didn't even know it. Now that I was on the other side, I was going to finally get the connection I had been needing.

CHAPTER **21**

 living for tomorrow
today

*Sing, sing a song. Make it simple to last the
whole life long.*

—THE CARPENTERS

Ain't no shame in being by yourself, but nobody was ever made to
be alone. Bernita was still living up north in Delaware, keeping to
herself. One night MaBisha talked her into going to a party that
Vernon Wilson, her UPS man, knew about. Now, things have
really changed. When I was young, black folks and white folks
weren't mixing at parties or nowhere else, but this party had some
of everybody. It was a good time too. They had music for listening
and music for dancing. There was all kinds of food and any kind
of card game you might want to get in on.

That party had somebody else there, it wasn't no coincidence.
Vernon had managed to convince Douglas to come to that gathering, but he wasn't having the fun that everybody else was. Douglas had a real hard time being in a crowded room. I'd almost say
that he had one of those phobias, but most black folks really don't

have the luxury of having fancy conditions. True, we all have somebody in our family that's a bit off, but that's all we call it. Them folks are still expected to do whatever it is they can do to contribute to the family.

Anyway, Vernon had begged Douglas to come, and he reluctantly agreed to meet him there. Douglas was sitting in a corner when Bernita walked in the door. He looked up and saw her and a feeling shot through him that caused him fear and joy at the same time. The joy was the same feeling he had had years before when he saw her for the first time. Douglas felt he knew Bernita from somewhere, but he wasn't quite sure where. He was smiling to himself when all of a sudden the fear hit. He didn't know what he was afraid of, but it was reminding him of the hurt he got from Venus. He bolted out of that party like he was Carl Lewis and when he got home he wrote a letter and turned it into another one of his paintings.

Back at the party, in a room off to the side, there was a woman who said she could read people. There was a line to get in to see her. She really did have a gift, but most people do. They just don't sit still long enough to tap into it. This woman's real gift wasn't for reading people, well, at least not the ones that were living.

The music was getting even better. They were playing the song that say "When love calls, you better answer. Don't let love slip away." Well, Vernon was looking like the song was written for him. He grabbed MaBisha and ran to the dance floor. MaBisha loved to dance. Vernon was real easy on the eyes but he couldn't find the beat if you handed it to him. They were sure nice to watch though. MaBisha was moving like she was born for dancing, and Vernon was just moving.

Bernita found a seat by the wall. She was watching and laughing when she heard somebody yelling her name.

"Bernita, Bernita Brown."

A tall dark woman was walking her way. Bernita recognized Lola immediately; her old college roommate who had introduced her to dirty rice. They hugged and laughed for what felt like a long time. Time don't really mean nothing on the other side, but when you see something good happening from over here, everything moves slow enough so we can watch the joy.

Bernita's mind went back to the time in her life when things were good. She could smell that rice that Lola made back in college again. This time though, it helped her to conjure up all the right memories. She thought about Mr. and Mrs. Morris and the love they showed her. She thought about the other girls from college and wondered how they'd made out. She thought of all the women she had helped and how many had come back to tell her so.

Bernita saw that her life had not been empty or wholly sad. She had been loved and she'd shown some love, too. Lola was smiling and talking through that smile.

"You look so happy," Lola said.

Bernita laughed. "I guess I am."

Bernita thought back to the night before when she had written herself another one of them letters. I 'd seen her writing it and I had to laugh.

Dear Self,

I am finally starting to seek after the life that I need and not the one that has been given to me. I know that God has plans for my life. They are plans of hope and not calamity. I know how the man in the Bible felt when he said, "Lord, I believe, but help my unbelief." I have had a hard time believing that God was hearing and helping me, but still I know that God is there. I am grateful for the things that I have gone through. I hope I can help others get through the storm.

   Now, it's time to dream and live.

   Me

Bernita was headed in the right direction, but you can still be on the right track and be on the wrong train.

   Lola pulled her friend toward the back room.

   "I have someone who wants to see you," Lola told her.

   Bernita would not have guessed that the someone was me.

   It turned out that the woman reading fortunes was Lola. She went past the line that had gotten longer.

   "I was next," a small angry woman said.

   "Your life will only get better when you stop hating yourself," Lola told her. "Now go and be happy."

   Bernita laughed. "Since when did you become a fortune teller?" she asked as they walked into the small room Lola had set up.

   "Oh, I'm not really," Lola said. "But whenever my husband throws a party, he likes for me to do my African women fortune-telling routine."

   Bernita was still smiling. She had forgotten how she felt when she first got free of her family. It was a good feeling and she had it again.

   "Can you really tell fortunes?" Bernita asked.

   "Sometimes," Lola said, smiling.

   Lola's room was decorated like you see in the movies. She had candles and incense burning. She even had a big crystal ball.

   "Well, what do you see in my future?" Bernita asked her.

   Lola smiled that smile of hers.

"It's not the future you need to be concerned with, my sister. You need to look into the past."

Bernita laughed but Lola didn't.

"Remember I told you I have someone for you to meet?" Lola asked.

Lola was sounding serious and Bernita was getting worried. She hoped that Lola hadn't met an old boyfriend or, worse still, her ex-husband.

"Look, Lo, I'm not waiting to meet anybody from my past. Let's just say it wasn't that bright."

"I know all about that, but this is important," Lola said. "I can't do it here because I need a few things."

Lola reached into a bag and handed Bernita a card.

"Can you meet me tomorrow at this address?" Lola asked her.

Bernita sure was curious, but she was a little bit scared too.

"Yeah, I guess so. What time?"

"How about midnight?" Lola said.

Bernita was getting up to leave.

"Lo, have you lost it? Why would we be meeting at midnight?"

"It will work better then," Lola said.

Lola was looking serious, so Bernita tried to do the same.

"I haven't seen you in over ten years and you want to meet me at some address on a card at midnight. You scaring me, Lo."

"It's nothing scary at all. I need to put you in touch with your Aunt Babe."

Well, you didn't even need a feather to knock Bernita over. If Lola hadn't caught her, she would have fallen down right on her behind. Bernita hadn't told any of her college sisters about her family. Whenever the subject came up, she turned quiet.

"How do you know my Aunt Babe?" Bernita asked. She was afraid to know, but needed to.

"There's a lot I need to explain and I can't do it here. I'll tell you tomorrow. It's so good to see you. We shall meet then, okay?"

It was more of a statement than a question, but Bernita said yes anyway.

CHAPTER 22

the meeting

If the living don't come to the dead, the dead will come to the living.

—AUNT BABE

There are rules for communicating with the dead, nothing too complicated though. It's a lot like talking to an elder. Speak when spoken to, show respect, don't walk away till you've been dismissed. There has always been an open line of communication between the living and the dead, but that line is used less and less frequently. Just like anything that is unused or abused, it starts to fade. Lots of folks get all spooked about talking to those who have crossed over. Hollywood has confused y'all into thinking that connecting with an ancestor is gruesome business. Native Americans used to commune so closely with us that folks felt that the Native Americans had to be done away with. All through the middle ages, people who they called witches got put to death for communing with nature and the ancestors. I'm a tell you true, the only thing wrong with communicating with us is not listening to the advice that's given.

Remember that story in the Bible about the man who died and wanted to go back and warn his family about the hereafter? He knew his kin had lived as badly as he had and he wanted to get them right. But God knew them folks wouldn't listen. They had been turning a deaf ear for centuries, so he wasn't 'llowed to return. Some folks think that because he couldn't cross over, nobody else can. Not so! That man was trying to change the natural course of reaping and sowing. He wanted his folks to be able to do whatever they was big enough to do and then switch tracks at the end of the road. No siree, Bob. Besides, wasn't none of his kin thinking 'bout him or any of their ancestors. That's what I'm getting at. It's important that you keep the line of communication open. Pay attention to the lives that have gone before, respect the contributions they made, and the work they did for you. If you don't, your life will be one empty mess; the more you try to do to fill it, the emptier you'll feel.

Lola had been listening to her ancestors since she was a child in Burkina Faso, over in Africa. Her family never thought it was strange that she could see and hear the dead. Most towns had at least one seer; Lola's had a mess of them. Even before she was born, the elders knew she was gonna be special. They also knew that she was gonna be traveling. Where she was from, the old people still had influence over the young. They would get together before a child was born and talk to God about who the baby was gonna be and how they should be named. The old folks knew that Lola was coming even before her parents did. They went to her mama and papa one day, laughing.

"She's coming, she's coming," the elders said.

Lola was born fussing like she had a lot to say. Everyone already understood that she was going to move away so they showered her with even more love than the children in the town normally got. Lola would need that love.

When she was ten, Lola's parents sent her to live with an uncle in the United States. He was married and had children of his own. Lola just became one more. For her people still in Africa, adding another child to your family was natural and normal. It used to be for us African-Americans in the United States too, but we have forgotten a lot of what we came here with.

Lola grew up like the rest of their kids, but she was still different. Sometimes she would sit for hours looking at something nobody else could see. Her uncle wasn't worried at all, but her aunt was American, so she didn't understand. Behind her husband's back, she took Lola to a head doctor. Well, of course, he thought the child had problems. They put her on some medicine that she stayed on all the way through college. Now you can say what you want, but drugs are drugs. I know from my own life that you can't put something into your body and not expect it to get into your spirit. Lola lost some of her light. But there was still a spark left. That was all the ancestors needed to start a fire.

It wasn't until she graduated from college that Lola remembered why she'd been sent here. Her purpose was to be a bridge between two worlds, the seen and unseen.

A few years after college, Lola got married to a Chinese doctor who took her off the medicine she had been taking all them years. When she stopped taking of them, she began to see things again like she had when she was little. She told her husband about it and he told his mother. Life sure is big, it's the world that's small. There were children just like Lola over in China too. Her mother-in-law knew all about them. Her grandmother had been one of them seers.

Lola finally learned to listen to what she had forgotten, and that's how she met me.

One day Lola had been going through some old pictures from her college days. Despite the medication, those days had been as good to her as they had been to Bernita. Her uncle and aunt were real nice to her growing up, but Lola had been downright spoiled back in Africa. Every home was full of children and laughter. When she got to college, she got some of that feeling back.

That day when she was looking at them old pictures, she found one of her and Bernita. She saw the sadness in Bernita's face and felt it in her own heart. She decided to start praying for Bernita right then. Now, folks will tell you if you think of somebody, the first thing you should do is get in touch with them. But the first thing gotta be prayer. Get in touch with God for them. Tell God how they made you feel and what you wanna see for their life.

That's what Lola did for Bernita. That was around the time that all that mess was going on at the Center. Now, you may have thought that Van trying to touch her was a terrible thing. That it was. But, if he hadn't done that, Bernita wouldn't have seen no reason to get out of there. When she left, a lot of other people could get out too. Lola's thoughts and prayers opened all of that up. She kept on praying for Bernita. She would write down her prayer and then she put it under a lit candle. This wasn't no hoodoo thing she was doing. No sir, no ma'am. What she did was light a candle in her own heart to remind herself to keep Bernita in constant prayer. Lots of times we think we need to go to somebody and tell them a bunch of what we feel. When people are at their lowest, it's hard for them to even hear what you gotta say. Better you talk to God.

Lola had been praying for Bernita and I was hearing them prayers. One day I tapped Lola on the shoulder, got her attention, and we been talking ever since. She was connected to my Bernita, so she was connected to me. Lola listened to us over here on the other side, so we talked to her. I wish I could have had that kind of time with Bernita. But time ain't everything, *timing* is.

Now, you been listening for a while, so don't get funny on me when I say this. There's a mess of them shows on where people talk to the dead. Some of it is for entertainment, and some of it is true. The memories of those who is gone ain't no big mystery. It's about life. Every generation is getting further and further away from the last. It was never meant to be like that. We was supposed to stay alive in your hearts so you could do more than we did.

Well, Lola felt me calling. She told me she was ready to hear. I told her all about me and it felt good. Now, sometimes folks want proof that all of this is real. All you gotta do is look at a baby's face. You'll see somebody who look like they been here before, even though you know they ain't. What you're looking at is the impression we left.

I was visiting Lola more and more. Sometimes we did party readings. They weren't nothing more than her repeating things that me and a couple others was telling her. I had a lot of fun doing that. I loved to see the look on the face of somebody when Lola would tell them something about their life that they knew she had no earthly way of knowing.

One day Lola told a woman that she was bringing shame on her family. This particular woman had been sleeping all over the place, just like I had done. That's why I knew just what to say.

Folks say that blood is thicker than water but when you get thirsty, you ain't wanting no blood to drink. We are connected through more than just blood and relations. The flow of life is like the flow of water; it moves where it will. That woman's life was connected to mine by what we both did 'cause we shared a common pain. Lola told her to stop before she joined up with somebody who would destroy her and her children's lives. That woman got to crying and thanking Lola for the truth.

Folks weren't always happy to hear about themselves though. Sometimes, when you are wrong, you don't want to hear about nothing right. It ain't just that folks don't like to be caught. They just don't want to stop what they were caught at. Whenever Lola ran into someone like that, I would warn her not to say too much. People have been killing women like Lola for as long as they've been around.

The night before, when Lola ran into Bernita was no accident. I told you MaBisha was on our side. Anybody who shows love and ain't trying to get something for theyself, is working for God. When MaBisha brought Bernita to that party, she was doing a mighty work.

That next night Lola got herself ready to meet with Bernita, but Bernita didn't show up. That didn't hurt Lola none. She just took the show to her.

The night before, when Bernita saw Lola and Lola got to talking about me, Bernita hid herself up in her house just like she had been doing with her life. When Lola rang her house buzzer over and over the next night, Bernita finally opened the door and let Lola in. Now, Lola didn't even ask why she hadn't shown up earlier. She ain't say a word about it. She sat down, pulled a candle out of her bag, and lit it. Bernita was just staring at her. Finally, Bernita said something.

"Why are you here?" Bernita asked.

Lola got to humming like she ain't hear her.

"Why are you here and what is this about really?"

Now them twin sisters, fear and disbelief, were working Bernita over something good. She was afraid to see her life and doubting herself at the same time.

"You have hidden your life under a bushel and it is time to come out. Love is calling you and it's time you answer," Lola told her.

Lola was serious, but she was smiling just the same.

"What do you know about my aunt?" Bernita asked. She had been afraid to come out and ask it, but her curiosity was getting the most of her. Lola smiled some more.

"I thought I would let her tell you herself," Lola said.

Well, I was never one to miss the chance to make an entrance.

Bernita sensed that something was happening. She closed her eyes in the hope that it was all a dream. When she finally opened them, I was sitting right next to her. Well, she jumped like she did the day old Van was trying to feel her up.

"This is not real, this is not real. Go away," Bernita was saying to me.

"It's one or the other, child. If I ain't real, how can I leave?" I asked her.

Bernita started to cry. She was shaking her head. "You are dead. My mama, Buster, she sent me the obituary from the paper."

I could feel Bernita remembering back to the day when she found out that I was dead. Buster never was much of a writer. The letter was short but not real sweet.

Dear Bernita,

Been trying to find you. It ain't been easy. I spoke with that teacher, Mr. Morris, and he gave me your address. Your Aunt Babe died, I thought you might want to know. You know where I am if you want to get in touch.

Buster, your mama

Bernita answered Buster's letter. Hearing about my death made her go back to the time when things were bad. The day she got that letter, she wrote one to me.

> *Dear Aunt Babe,*
>
> *I wish you had a chance to know me as an adult. Maybe then you would have liked me. I don't know why you hated me so, but I do know that it had something to do with not having anyone to really love you. I remember that you had lots of men though. It's funny how a person can have a lot of sex, but very little love. I guess I shouldn't judge, I've haven't had much of either. I hope that you got a chance to have redemption.*
>
> *Your niece,*
> *Bernita*

I was thinking back on that letter from Bernita. I knew that I had caused a lot of pain, and I knew that I had a lot to do with why Bernita was going from pillar to post trying to find love.

I told her I was glad to see that Buster cared enough about me and her to send that letter. "I saw the one you wrote too," I told her, "and I understand you now. I'm here to help."

"This is a trick. You can't be real," Bernita said, and started hugging herself and rocking like she always did when she was nervous.

"You know I'm real, you just don't want to know. I can't stay long so you need to listen to me good."

Bernita was crying and rocking harder and faster. "No, no, no, no, no."

"Look," I was talking real stern 'cause I needed her to listen and remember. "I want you to know that I love you, and I apologize for what I did and what I didn't do."

Well, something about love can stop a person dead in they tracks. Pardon the expression if you will. Bernita had gone through a life without love and now I was trying to give her what I should have given her when she was young.

"How dare you!" Bernita said. She stood up and faced me like she had when she was a child. "I have tried to get away from you and your life for years. Now you come in here with my friend like it's okay, and I'm supposed to do what, love you back? What good would that do?"

Bernita got up, blew out the candle, and walked to her bedroom. She yelled back to Lola and told her to let herself out.

the cleansing

An open heart is easily wounded and hard to repair.

—ANONYMOUS

Bernita didn't go to sleep right away. She was in that room telling herself that none of this was real. Bernita had made herself believe that she was having one of them nervous breakdowns. Ain't it something how folks can finally find what they need but think that they done gone and lost it. You've been swimming in mess so long that the goodness don't look like nothing you want. Well, I whispered in her head and told her to be calm and she finally got some sleep. Bernita slept through the night. I knew she was gonna need it.

She woke up feeling better than she had in a long time. She was actually humming. I let her get up and get washed. I even waited till she got through with breakfast.

"Good morning, this morning; how you doing this fine morning?" I asked.

Well, who told me to say that? Bernita let out one of them screams like they do in all them crazy movies. It wasn't that loud, but if you were looking at her face, you'd a thought that she had seen a ghost. But I guess that's right, she had. I still have a hard time remembering that's how the living see us. We ain't nothing more than memories.

I let Bernita scream a bit more before I tell her to hush. If she wanted some freedom from the pain of her life, she was gonna have to go back up in there to get it. That's why the Sankofa bird looks back over his shoulder. He's showing us that the way out is back through.

"You need to quit all that noise and face yourself," I said. "Last night I told you I love you. But you don't want to hear it. So what is it that you would like to know?"

Bernita stopped crying right then. She was getting madder and madder, and that was okay too. The Bible say to get angry but sin not. The question that should come to mind is, Why would God say it's all right to get angry? Well, since I'm dead and you ain't, I'll just tell you. God wants you to get angry enough to change the situation, but not to destroy it. When Bernita was done being scared and started getting mad, she was going from "I can't do anything" to "I better do something."

"Why are you here?" Bernita asked. She had her hand on her hip just like she did when she first told me off all them years back. "Don't tell me how it's because you love me. You're the last person I want to hear that from."

I smiled 'cause I like to deliver hard words with a soft expression.

"Oh yeah, who would you rather it be from? You looking for Tyrone, Jimmymack, old Re Member, or would you like to see Van and Tricia?" I asked her.

"How dare you, you filthy old—" Bernita said.

Now she was stepping over into the sin area. But I ain't back up none. I know that she was used to taking whatever she got and still doing the right thing. Maybe she needed to have a little bad fun. God knows, she ain't had too much of no kind of fun in her life.

"You come here calling the names of the few men I've been with. You were with more men than I can ever name."

I told Bernita that her trouble wasn't in the numbers and neither was mine.

"You seem to know so much about me," Bernita said. She was standing up now. "Why don't you tell me what my trouble *is*?"

I kept on smiling 'cause now I could see she was gonna get somewhere. I didn't say nothing. I gave her enough space to fill in her own blanks. If somebody is getting all uppity with you, hold your peace and your words. Look them straight in the face and don't answer nothing. Watch and see how crazy it'll make them. When folks can't make you answer they nonsense, they gonna have to answer it for themselves.

Well, Bernita got to walking and saying how all she had ever tried to do was be loved. What was the harm in that? She wanted to know why she couldn't get no love. All the right she did for folks was thrown back in her face. When she was done getting mad, she was tired. She was crying when she looked up and said, "I just want to be loved."

If I didn't know better, I would have been feeling sorry for Bernita. But I did know better, so my feelings didn't have no place.

"It's been here all along," I tell her. "Get up out of your pain and go get some love."

I said that and left. Or as the young people say, I got ghost.

That night Bernita wrote one of her best letters yet.

Dear Me,

I don't know what's happening, but I feel like I'm losing my mind and yet gaining it all at the same time. I had a visit from my dead Aunt Babe. And as you know, I don't like to deal with my past. But now, I know that I have to. My aunt has a lot to do with why I am the way I am. When I was a girl, she was the most beautiful person I knew. When she smiled, it was like the sun had come for a visit. But then she changed. As I grew older, she became bitter and angry toward me and I never understood why. One day, she beat me so badly that I could not breathe. I want to understand her and my mother as well, but I am afraid of opening that door. I don't really know what I may find. If I am to move forward with my life, I know that I have to look back into my past. I'm not so sure that I'm ready.

Me

Bernita didn't understand it yet, but she was preparing herself to be free. She took to talking to herself and to me. This went on for days till she was talking her way back around to what she needed to do. She was talking and I was hearing, but I wouldn't show up for her. Bernita needed to get her own life in order. You can't live for nobody and can't nobody live for you.

During that period of time, Bernita was just going to work at the Passage Way House and coming home. She didn't do nothing else. She was still in the land of the living, but she wasn't living. She knew all kinds of scriptures, but knowing them and living them ain't one and the same. When she had left the Center, she tried to leave God too. Why is it that when man messes up, God gotta take the blame? After she left that place, Bernita stopped reading the Bible. She was still praying 'cause once you done talked to God, you can't never stop. One day, out of somewhere, Bernita got the notion to pick up the Bible again. She fell into Job and got to reading about all Job went through. It made good sense to her, 'cause Job's life felt like her own. She was thinking the same way Job did, that God was responsible for all of her pain. Well, that wasn't the whole truth. And if you ain't got the whole truth, you ain't got none of it. God allowed them things to happen to Job, but God didn't cause them.

Well, Bernita read on to the place where Job got his life back better than it had been. Before Job got all of his life and stuff back better than it was, the Bible say he forgave his friends, the ones who came and told him that God had caused all of this pain because of something he had done. Job hadn't done nothing and he didn't think he did neither. When you living right, and right comes to you, people who ain't doing the same can't do nothing but be mad about it. Well, Job forgave them for the pain they caused and everything came back, only better. Forgiveness is as powerful as it is simple.

Now that I'm over on the other side, I know a few things that I didn't know when I was alive. You got to take inventory from time to time. Go back over your life and look at the people who you think done you wrong. Forgive them and then forgive yourself.

I ain't telling you to go and call them and let them back up in your life. When you finally seeing why your life is how it is, don't go back to the mess that made it that way. I been through plenty of men, but I ain't never gone back to none of them. That's one of the good things I passed down to Bernita. I gave her the strength to not look back over her leaving.

Leaving was something she learned for herself.

When Bernita reached that simple truth in Job, she got to crying. She got up from where she was reading and lit a candle. Then she sat down in front of it and was thinking on all of the folks who had hurt her. The more she thought about us, the more that candle flickered. She lined up all them same people I had named before. She looked at Tyrone Phillip Thomas and remembered the terrible time he put her through. All of his lying and stealing came back to her. It felt as bad then as it did the first time. She looked at how he treated her in bed and how she learned to hate her body and herself. She got to feeling real weak. Bad thoughts bring bad feelings. The mind and spirit live in your body. What happens to one will happen to the other. Bernita got a pain in her chest to match the one in her spirit. She wanted to hate him but she thought of old Job.

"I forgive you, Tyrone."

She said it softly at first and then she got louder with each turn. The more she said it the more she believed it. As she grew in her faith, she got a clear picture of Tyrone and how he came to be the way he was. It's a blessing to really be able to feel free of somebody. Bernita got to see Tyrone when he was a boy and she saw why he was the way he was.

A man who sold soft pretzels and candy would go around from house to house taking orders for his stuff. Everybody liked him on account of how he would watch people's kids if they wanted him to. One day he watched pretty Tyrone. He touched Tyrone's privates and made Tyrone touch his too. Tyrone never forgot that. When he was getting older, he found that he liked to cook and make things. His sorry relatives called him names. The only person Tyrone knew of who was what they were calling a "sissy" and a "fag" was the pretzel man. That man wasn't no good. He was a crook. He tried to steal something from Tyrone that he didn't want to give. Now, you gotta hear me good on this. Some men grow up to like other men 'cause of what was done to them. But some are just that way. They ain't doing it out of pain. Take my sister Buster. She got to loving other women 'cause it was a woman who showed her love. Tyrone Phillip Thomas might have loved men on his own, but because that grown man forced little Tyrone to do something he shouldn't have, later on Tyrone had a hard time figuring out who he was and what he truly wanted. Since he couldn't love hisself, he tried to destroy anybody who loved him.

In her prayer and meditation, Bernita saw all of why Tyrone was the way he was plus something else. She saw the two roads that were the choices for his life. Tyrone had taken the lesser road, but that didn't matter none.

Every life has two major roads; one that's divine and one that's secondary. That secondary road is the one you take when you just looking for a shortcut. God really does mean for us to have life and have it more abundantly, it's a tougher journey though. Now, that secondary road ain't bad, it's just one of them "it'll do's." That's what you take when you don't get what you really want. My life wasn't even a secondary road. I got lost and ended up on a back alley.

Bernita went on down her lineup and got to sending forgiveness to the others. Jimmymack needed a whole bunch of love. God don't make anybody ugly. We do that ourselves. You've seen those people who got features that don't look like they fit each other. They can have big noses and lips and little everything else, and there will still be some beauty about them. Jimmymack could have been on that road. Instead, he chose to believe what most people said about him. I said most, because no matter how bad the situation seem, it don't mean all. Jimmymack's grandmother always told him to be nice.

"Jimmy, you ain't what some folks call pretty, but you are beautiful," Jimmy's grandmother said.

Jimmy had been crying on account of some kids were calling him names and telling him he needed a bag over his head.

"You act good and you will look good. But if you act bad, no matter how good you look, you'll still be ugly."

Well, Jimmy acted good and he was looking good. But because he was so nice and worked hard, he made decent money, which he hardly ever spent. The first woman he attracted liked his money and ways more than she liked him. She took advantage of Jimmy but he kept on loving her. Ain't no harm in going in the wrong door. It's when you move in that sets life in a mess. Jimmy kept on loving that greedy, needy woman till she took all of his nice. Jimmy took that pain out on everybody except the one who hurt him. To make matters worse, she was the one who walked out on him. Had it been the other way around, she might not have still had a hold on him.

When somebody treat you bad and then walk out on you, you feel more inclined to try to win them back. Even when you know things ain't right, you still think you got something to prove. If you in something that's real bad, find the strength to leave. That way, when it's your choice, you can still be in control.

Well, Jimmymack wasn't the one to leave, so whenever that woman came sniffing around, he fell right back into his bed of pain. When he met Bernita, things could've been right for them both, but each of them had mess caked on their shoes from the last trip.

Bernita saw what happened to Jimmymack and she prayed for him too. She prayed that God would allow him to remember and appreciate the truth he'd heard from his grandmother.

When she got to Re Member, Bernita had to laugh. She was tickled by what she had put up with. She saw that white boy in all the African robes talking Swahili who told her that she wasn't being herself. She prayed again and forgave him. She sent him the power to believe in hisself and to love and connect with the person he really was.

"And Lord," Bernita prayed, "help him remember that his name is not Re Member."

When Bernita was done praying, she put her thoughts into a plan. She wrote a letter that was full of *her* desires and *her* goals.

My Dearest Bernita,

For a long time you have walked in the will and wishes of others. Now, it's time that you start to live for yourself. I plan to find the right kind of love for me. I don't need to respond to the first person who comes by. I am beautiful and wonderful. I have the right to choose the kind of love I need. Now that I realize this, I can see that I have given very little thought to my own desires. I will now, because I know that I should.

Here is my list of love requirements. I don't know who he is, but somehow, I feel that he's on his way to me.

- *My Love must have a sense of humor*
- *My Love must have a strong sense of himself*
- *My Love must be beautiful (I must be able to feel it and see it)*
- *My Love must be crazy about me, but not too crazy*

That's all for now. I'll add to this list from time to time.

P.S.

I love me

Bernita read over her letter and got to laughing so hard that she barely heard the phone ringing. She caught it before it went to that machine of hers. "Hey, Bernisha, I was just thinking 'bout you. I miss you, girl," Jimmymack said.

Bernita had to work hard to talk. She knew that the call wasn't no accident. She was starting to see the power she had. She chatted with Jimmy for a while, and she told him that she was happy to hear from him. Well, Jimmy asked her to forgive him and Bernita cried and said yes. Then my girl showed me what she was made of. When Jimmy asked if he could take her out sometime, she stopped and thought about it. Bernita told Jimmy she was glad to hear from him, but that she didn't think it would be a good idea to get together. And that's right where she left it and him; in the past where they belonged.

CHAPTER 24

ceremony of forgiveness

We have circled and circled till we have arrived
at home again, we too.

—WALT WHITMAN

As soon as Bernita put the phone down, it rang again. Forgiveness sure do travel fast. She was afraid it was gonna be her ex-husband or Re Member. She almost didn't answer, but she made up her mind to face whatever was coming head on. When she braced herself, her body tensed right up.

"Hello?" It was more of a question than a greeting. "That you?" MaBisha asked. She was sounding real good to Bernita. She always did but there was a lot more joy in her voice than before.

"Boy, am I glad it's you," Bernita said.

"Who were you expecting? You doing something I don't know about?" MaBisha asked.

Bernita laughed and told MaBisha about the call she got from Jimmymack. She didn't tell her about me. Some things need to be done slowly and in person.

"Lord child, don't bring that roughneck back around," Ma-Bisha said.

Bernita told her she didn't plan on it.

"Hey before I forget, I got good news and bad news."

MaBisha believed in balance. I sure did like her.

"You know the way, let me down so you can pull me back up," Bernita told her.

"Bad news is I'm gaining weight and gonna be gaining a whole lot more. The good news is I'm pregnant."

Bernita started screaming and so did MaBisha. They were both in their thirties now. Bernita had gone through her childbearing years using every protection device she could find. She had been in too many painful relationships to think about bringing a child into one. More recently though, Bernita had been wishing that she'd had at least one child, then she could have had someone to give her love to.

MaBisha's other children were in college or on their own. This baby was like a surprise birthday party. You don't know you're getting one, but you kind of expect it. When everybody yells surprise, you're sure glad.

Bernita and MaBisha talked for two hours. They were like teenage girls. They planned and talked, when it hit Bernita.

"So you and Vernon going to get married?" Bernita asked.

MaBisha sighed. "You know he's been asking me to. Vernon is an only child, he's really into the whole family thing. I want to, kind of. But . . . "

"But what?" Bernita wanted to know.

Bernita wasn't trying to get too far in her friend's business. She just wanted to make sure that MaBisha was getting all she could out of life. Somebody should.

"Well, if you must know, Bernita, I'm afraid," MaBisha said.

"My ex-husband was everything I had dreamed of, or so I thought. Who knew he was really a nightmare?"

"Yeah, but every cloud has a silver lining," Bernita told her. She was passing on things she had only just now learned herself. Go on, girl!!!

"Look at it this way," Bernita said. "If your husband hadn't beat the crap out of you, we wouldn't have met. If we hadn't met, you wouldn't be having a baby with the best-looking man that ever drove a delivery truck."

MaBisha was smiling now. "I know everything happens for a reason. I'm just scared."

Bernita talked and joked a little more, then she told her friend about Job.

"Send your ex the forgiveness he needs, and release yourself from the pain he caused you. He has moved on with his life, it's time for you to move on with yours."

MaBisha said thank you and went to do what she was told.

Several hours later Bernita's phone rang again. This time it was MaBisha's friend Vernon. He was calling to say thanks and to tell Bernita to get ready to party because there was going to be a wedding. Bernita screamed and laughed with Vernon like he was one of her girlfriends too. Love will bring you into the fold, without ever making a crease. When MaBisha tried to grab the phone from Vernon to talk to Bernita, Vernon ran around the room.

"She's my friend too, can't I talk to Bernita without you butting in?" Vernon said, smiling. "Ya'll talked all about me for the longest time, now it's my turn to talk about you."

Bernita could hear MaBisha whining and laughing at the same time. Her friend had finally met her match.

When love comes, it hits everyone that's connected to the love.

Bernita was feeling like she was getting a brother, and Vernon knew that he had a new sister. They laughed and talked until Bernita finally told Vernon that he'd better go and celebrate with his fiancée.

When Vernon hung up the phone, his joy reminded him to share the good news with *his* best man. Life sure is wonderful. It connects back to itself and gives you one big old hug. Vernon and Douglas had been good friends for going on ten years. They were different as they could be, but they had a sameness that ran to the core.

Well, when Vernon told Douglas that he was getting married, Douglas laughed and cried. I love it when men do that. Then he told Douglas that he was going to be a father and Douglas went to crying some more. Good feelings gave way to embarrassment, and them boys got off the phone. When the people you love get happy from love, it can make you real hopeful. Douglas went to put them good feelings on a canvas. His paintings had become his way of writing the letters me and his daddy encouraged him to write.

Douglas painted a rose that opened up into full bloom. In the center of that rose was an eye. The eye dripped a single tear onto the rose. Standing behind the rose was the woman who that eye belonged to. Don't you know that boy had painted my Bernita!

Life was giving me another one of its hugs. Douglas sprayed something over that painting to make it dry a bit and then he painted the words:

> *My dear come near*
> *Step through our fear*
> *And into my heart.*

facing yourself

Life ain't been no crystal stair. But all the while,
I's still a climbing.

—LANGSTON HUGHES

When MaBisha got her joy, Bernita was getting some too. Bernita was humming and cooking dinner when it dawned on her that she hadn't forgiven the man who had caused her the most pain. Being hurt by somebody you loving is one thing, but to get it from somebody who supposed to be talking for God, well, that's another kind of mess. Soon as old Van came into Bernita's head, all her humming stopped. She got dizzy. She steadied herself, took a deep breath, and got a glass of water.

Bernita got the air and water she needed, and it was time for her to light the fire. She lit a candle and prayed. She thanked God for her life and the things she had been able to endure. Then she asked to be forgiven for all the times she had stepped off her path. Then she made a mental picture of Van and told him that she was forgiving him for what he did. In her head, she stood there big as life next to Van, and she added Tricia to the picture. She said, "I forgive you" three times and blew out her candle. When she did I was sitting on the other side of the room.

"Hey, Bernita Brown. You sure are a fast learner," I said.

Bernita smiled at me and gave a little laugh. This time she wasn't afraid, but she wasn't ready to forgive me just yet.

"Hey yourself, Aunt Babe. You looking mighty good for a dead woman."

"It's the peace," I told her. "It looks good on me. Besides, you just seeing me the way I was meant to be, not how I turned out."

"To what do I owe the pleasure?" Bernita asked.

Now it was my turn to laugh. "Not to what my dear, to whom?"

Bernita stopped smiling.

"There's somebody else you need to forgive," I said.

She had done a lot that day. I wished I could've given her more time, but on earth, it really does run out.

"Yeah," Bernita said. "I know."

Bernita took a deep breath and got ready to say what she wanted to. "I need to forgive you."

"And your mama, and yourself. Look, Bernita." I said the rest of what I needed to say fast, 'cause I could feel my move coming. "There's a lot more life you got coming to you," I told her, "and it can't come if you all balled up. You gotta open up so light can pour in."

Bernita's tears came streaming down her face. She was looking just like the little child that I used to drag around when I was doing my dirt, back when I was just a child myself. Bernita could see that now. She was starting to remember all the things she needed to know.

Bernita chose to forgive her mama first. She looked back to her childhood and saw her mother standing there.

Bernita could see her child self wishing and hoping to make her mother stay with her. She saw all the good she did trying to get her mother's attention, and she saw how nothing worked. Then she remembered how she gave up trying and lived for herself.

Bernita cried and the tears of relief poured down her face and onto her neck. One of them tears dropped down to the wall around her heart. That one tear washed all that pain away.

Then Bernita said them simple words and more life came back to her.

"I forgive you, Mommy."

She had never called Buster that, so hearing it did something to me, too.

When forgiveness comes, it shines a light on the truth.

Bernita got to see some of Buster's pain and how empty her life had been. The only man Buster was ever with was Bernita's father. She didn't love him, but he'd tried. When he told her, she just laughed and walked off. She'd got what she wanted, and didn't need him for anything else. There are a whole mess of women who will sleep with a man hoping to get pregnant. Some do it for money, some to trap them, then there are some who do it just for the child. That was Buster. One of my other sisters told Buster that since she was *that* way, she was never going to have a baby. Buster bet her three dollars that she would have one and do it before her. Buster won, but Bernita didn't. There are a lot of children who are born for even sadder reasons, but that was sad enough.

Bernita was rocking and crying. She saw that the only person Buster really loved had loved her back, but Miss Eudora died a day after Bernita left. Buster hadn't loved anybody again. She was still down in Sylvania living a loveless life. She wrote to Bernita from time to time, and Bernita would write her back. But there was never a bit of emotion in none of those letters. Bernita could see that this was all Buster could do. She was crying, but her heart was happy when she said, "I do forgive you, Mommy, and I love you."

Bernita lit another candle and kneeled down in front of it.

That's when Bernita got to me. Forgiveness can never come too late. Bernita got a feeling of pain, then relief, and that turned into joy. If I had had a body, I would have been feeling it too. It was powerful enough to see through her.

Then Bernita did the magic.

"I forgive you, Aunt Babe. When I was a girl I looked up to you. You looked like a beautiful bird. Everyone wanted to be with you, even if it was temporary. You had a light but you thought it was the sex that attracted men. I saw your light and I wanted nothing more than to be like you. I used to think that you took me around because you loved me so much. When I got older, I could see the real reason. I was nothing more than bait for you to lure some man who didn't even deserve to be with you. You didn't need me for that, Aunt Babe. Anybody would have wanted you. The day you beat me was nothing in comparison to what you had already done to me. But I forgive you because I know now that you weren't doing nothing to me, you were doing it to yourself."

If I could have cried, I would have. Instead, I smiled on the inside, 'cause this was victory. Bernita got to see my life and with it came her own. She lit another candle and said what she was needing to say most.

"I forgive you, Bernita, for being afraid to just be."

I was starting to fade. When you forgive us for what we did in life, you can move on and so can we.

CHAPTER 26

the secret of success

She who dwells in a secret place shall abide in the temple of the most high.

—PSALMS 91:1

I kept watching Bernita the way I always did. Whenever Bernita wanted to think on me, she would be able to get the answers she needed from my life.

The day she stepped into forgiveness was the beginning of her real life's journey. She called up her old friend Lola and invited her over.

The two girls got together and laughed like they were back in school. It was easier for Bernita to see Lola now that she had dealt with me. The first time they got together was scary and uneasy. This time was for fun. Lola went through Bernita's icebox and came up with enough stuff to make a real good batch of dirty rice. They ate and talked some more. Lola told Bernita about her life during the years they had been apart. Bernita shared hers. They laughed about what they called their "man mistakes." The more they talked, the less guilt Bernita felt for what somebody had done to her. A lot of the pain is caused by silence. When Bernita told Lola about Van, she got real serious and still.

"This person must be dealt with," Lola told her.

"I already prayed for him." Bernita was ready to let bygones be, but Lola wasn't.

"That's good, because he's going to need it," Lola said.

For all Bernita knew, that was the end of it. That night after she had gone home, Lola made a circle on the floor in white chalk. She got in the center of that circle and thought back over generations. She saw others in the tribe who, like her, were able to see beyond the physical. She asked them for guidance. The answer came through them into her thoughts. Now before you go getting spooked on me, let me tell you this; Lola wasn't working roots. Roots is when you trying to control the will of others to get to something you want for yourself. Lola was going to set a wrong right. Van and Tricia and all the others like them had used goodness against good people.

Lola prayed for the natural balance of life to be restored to those who had been hurt by the Vans and Tricias. There were many. As she prayed, Van and Tricia were touched and that night they both dreamed of all the lives they'd tried to hurt. In a lot of cases they succeeded. In some they didn't. Then the dream turned into a nightmare. They saw that most of the people they tried to destroy were doing better than they were. That was more than enough. When they woke up, they set out to do to each other what they had tried to do to everybody else.

CHAPTER 27

the trial

Scratch that out of the air and put it in your heart.
—JEANINE CHAMBERS

MaBisha and Vernon sure did throw some kind of wedding. It didn't take a lot of time or money. They held it at the same place where Bernita reunited with her old friend Lola. MaBisha and Vernon called all of their friends the week before and told them to come and bring a dish. Seems like everybody that had been to the shelter was there. MaBisha had told them to bring their children too. That sure did make the party even nicer. Some people think of children as a burden, but they got things all wrong.

MaBisha and Vernon had a real short marriage ceremony. The minister was a man who volunteered at the shelter, driving the women back to their houses to pick up what they needed. Gus was a big man and a retired policeman to boot.

A lot of the men would be yelling and swearing at their wives until they saw Gus get out of the car. He would walk over to them and tell them that they could do it easy or they could do it hard. The choice was theirs. There was only one fellow who chose hard. That man had grabbed his wife by the hair and got ready to hit her. Next thing he knew, he was waking up in the same hospital he put his wife in the week before.

Gus in his preaching robe was a sight for everybody who knew him. He talked about the gift of love and how it could heal all pain. He told Vernon and MaBisha that life was short, but love would last forever.

"The love you show each other will last beyond your years," Gus said. "I would pronounce y'all husband and wife, but God did that when he brought y'all together. So, I guess you should just kiss."

Well, folks was laughing and crying all at the same time. There wasn't nothing formal about that wedding, but it was better than the ones that people spend a fortune on. People ate and danced all night long. It sure was a good time. Best thing of all though was something that almost didn't happen. But love sure does conquer all.

The night of the wedding, Bernita was doing her usual thing of sitting by the wall. People were trying to get her up to dance, but she told them she was fine. Well, she was watching the dance floor when out of somewhere else come this beautiful soul named Douglas Ford. He looked good enough to drive.

Now I really do have to move back so you can catch up. I told you that old Douglas and Vernon were good friends, and you know that me and Douglas's dead daddy Ray have been hanging out, so to speak. Well, there's more I need to tell you.

You don't ever just run into somebody, and you never meet anybody by chance. Everyone is connected, but some are closer than others because they have an ancestral link. That link is why you keep meeting some of the same folks over and over again. Think about it for a moment and then get happy. Think about all of the folks who came to America during slavery. They were pulled away form their family and loved ones, but they only lost touch in this life. They were reconnected in the next. That connection is still going on today. The next time you're in a crowded place, look around you. You will always see people who will remind you of someone else. Over on this side, we make sure that you have a way of linking up with your people even if you don't know it. You gotta be careful how you treat folks. You don't know how connected they may be to your own self. You can't stand around mad at white people just 'cause they white. They may be a relative, or something more; they could be the descendent of a person who helped your ancestors get to freedom. Sometimes we put folks back together so they can get the thank-you they need to hear. On the other hand, the very one you think is fine 'cause they what you call "your people," may be the very one you should be running from.

You connect to others for a reason. We ancestors make the connection happen; it's up to you to figure out the reason.

Right around the time Bernita was meeting me, Douglas was meeting Ray. Now, if you think Bernita had a hard time meeting me, you should have seen old Douglas. The boy had been working hard at becoming a hermit, so he didn't really want to meet nobody, alive or dead. He was still driving for the delivery company every now and again when he felt like he needed the inspiration. The boy actually paid his boss to let him drive when he wanted to. I ain't lying. That chile was making real good money as an artist, but you would not have known it to see him. He moved into a nicer place, but that was all he did when all that money was coming in. He rarely socialized, but he stayed close to Vernon. Me and Ray made sure of that.

One day, Vernon was able to get Douglas out of the house. They went to lunch and to a ballgame. At the game, Vernon noticed a man with his young son. He told Douglas that he was looking forward to moments like that one. They sat staring at that father and son. It was a strong moment, but as soon as somebody scored a point they went to cheering like that sweet moment never happened. Men are like that. They don't linger over touchy moments like women do. They don't want nobody to think they too sensitive. Anyway, something about that moment made Douglas wonder about how his life would have been if he'd known his father. Later on that evening, he put them thoughts on canvas. Well, that's all that Ray needed to make his connection. He didn't go to Douglas like I did with Bernita; he sent his sister Marie. She called Douglas out of the blue and told Douglas that she was his relation. Now, Douglas was getting a reputation on account of his art was all over the place. He figured that this woman was just another nut who was trying to cash in, but the woman talked long enough to let him know that she was telling the truth.

"I don't want anything from you," she said, "but I have some things you need to have."

Two days later, Douglas got a package that set his life into high gear. There were some pictures of his father and one of his mother and father together. Turns out, old Ray from Around the Way could write a mean letter. There was one written to Douglas's mother. I know that you want to know what it said, and I'm gonna tell you, but I'll have to get back to that in a bit. First, let me tell you about how Bernita and Douglas met.

That day at the wedding, Douglas walked right up to Bernita

like he was used to meeting women. There is something about a man with a purpose.

"Can I sit here or do I need to fight somebody?" he asked her.

Bernita looked over to see all the handsome that had sat down. She was liking what she was seeing. Then she remembered that looks had gotten her in big trouble before. He was confident, and Bernita liked that, but Tyrone Phillip Thomas had been too.

"There's nobody to beat but me," Bernita said. She was smiling with her face, but her spirit was giving off that whole "leave me alone" thing she had learned so well.

"My name is Douglas Ford. I used to work with Vernon, he's a good friend of mine. Are you a friend of MaBisha's?"

Bernita liked the sound of Douglas's voice but she didn't like the way he was making her feel. When the tone and timbre of a man's voice gets all up in your head, it can do things to you down in the lower parts of your body. Well, Bernita wasn't having none of it, but she was still too nice to be rude. All this man did was make her feel good. Why should she punish him for that?

"My name is MaBisha—I mean, I'm a friend of Bernita's. Oh Lord," Bernita said, trying hard not to blush.

"That's okay," Douglas was really smiling now. "When I first saw you, I couldn't talk either."

"I see you two finally met." Vernon said after he and MaBisha danced over. Good thing they did, 'cause Bernita was having a hard time coming up with something to say to Douglas.

"See, 'Bisha, I told you they would like each other. MaBisha thought Douglas was too shy for you, Bernita. And look how you two have found each other on your own."

Bernita laughed. "If he's shy, I'm white."

Douglas's laugh was more like a song. It made everybody else laugh too.

"I introduced Bernita to the me nobody knows, but I guess she didn't like him," Douglas told them.

"Give her time," MaBisha said. "I had to."

They danced off to another table but Vernon turned around and gave a thumbs up.

Bernita was feeling like she had been talked about and set up, and she didn't care for it either. She tried to get up again but Douglas caught her hand.

"Please don't leave me," he told her.

There was something familiar in the way he said it.

"What would happen if I did?" Bernita asked him.

Douglas's voice and now his hand were getting the best of my Bernita.

"I don't think I'll be able to go on," Douglas said. He could not have looked any more truthful if he had been trying to, but Bernita looked at him like he had just told her a lie. Everything he said was true. But when you used to bad, good can seem false. Bernita got up and this time she did leave. Douglas didn't do nothing to stop her.

How is it that folks can wait their whole life for something only to turn away from it when it when it finally does come? You don't need to answer. That's what they call a rhetorical question. Bernita met up with love, but she made the choice to run back up into herself. She was hiding from beauty and happiness. MaBisha's wedding should have been a happy day for Bernita too. It would have been if it wasn't for Douglas Ford. There was something about him that made her nervous, but all I could do was watch. I had given her all the help she needed.

Douglas Ford wasn't done with Bernita. He couldn't get her off his mind. He waited a full twenty-four hours before he called on his old friend for help.

"Hey, Vern. This is Doug. How's married life?"

Vernon was smiling. He was married to a strong, wonderful woman and they were going to have a child.

"Man, any better and I'm going to have to write a musical," Vernon said.

"Ooh! Can I be you and will you get MaBisha's friend to play her?" Douglas asked. Douglas could always speak his mind with Vern. It wasn't that way with everyone.

When MaBisha first met Douglas, she asked Vernon how the two of them ever got along. "He don't even talk much," MaBisha told Vernon.

"Oh, he talks when nobody is around," he said.

Whenever Douglas came over and MaBisha was around, Douglas wouldn't say anything, so after a couple of times, MaBisha learned to just leave the two of them together. The first time Vernon suggested to MaBisha that Douglas should meet Bernita, she told him to think again.

"I wouldn't do that to somebody I *don't* like. He's weird," she said.

But Vernon kept telling Douglas about Bernita. But he also told him that MaBisha thought he was too shy. That's why Douglas showed himself the way he did at the wedding.

If MaBisha had taken the time to get to know old Douglas, she would have been able to see how much he and Bernita had in common. Outside of work, Bernita was really shy too. Just because you outgoing in one arena, don't mean that you are in all of them.

Vernon laughed, but told Douglas that he felt for him.

"Everybody should find love. There's somebody out there for you," Vernon said.

"I found her, Vern, and I want her bad."

Vernon couldn't believe that this was his friend. He thought the only thing Douglas had ever really needed was to do his art.

"You got it bad," Vernon told him.

"Yeah, man I really do," Douglas said. "I don't know what she put on me, but I ain't really been able to work."

Now, I knew something that Vernon didn't. He didn't know that Douglas had met Bernita before. Douglas didn't even remember it himself. And he didn't know that me and Ray had been working up to this moment for some time, but like the Bible say, all things work together for good.

I decided to give old Douglas a nudge. It didn't take much. He was real receptive. Now, if you ever meet an artist who ain't too spiritual, you better not buy they art. Mind you, I didn't say religious. I'm talking about the ability to connect on a level that goes beyond the here and now. Well, I got to telling Douglas that he needed to know Bernita. I let him see that there was more to her than she was letting him see. He told Vernon that he needed to have another meeting with Bernita.

"Can you make it happen, bro?" Douglas sounded real desperate.

"I sure will," Vernon told him.

CHAPTER 28

getting back up on the horse

If you can look up, you can get up.

—WILLIE JOLLEY

Bernita went back to living her day-in-day-out life. She did everything the way she had been doing it all along, but she felt better doing it. When you forgive people, it really does set you free. But the thing that really made her life more interesting was Douglas Ford. She thought about him and how his voice made her feel. She played his words over and over and tried to tell herself that she was wasting her thoughts. MaBisha and Vernon had left for their honeymoon a few days after the wedding. The wedding may have been quick and cheap, but the trip MaBisha took with her husband was far from that. They went to Egypt, Tanzania, and Madagascar. I sure would have liked to do all that when I was alive. Me and Goody had talked about traveling. We would've got to it if I hadn't made my exit from the land of the living so soon. MaBisha enjoyed herself something good. This was a woman who knew how to open the door for joy.

Bernita was getting postcards from all over Africa, but she really needed to talk to her friend. Maybe she'd been too hard on Douglas Ford. Then again, maybe she hadn't. She would have to wait for MaBisha to get back to ask her. In the meantime she had her thoughts.

Time and season play a big part in how well we live. If you plant something before its time, don't expect to get no good yield. Vernon had told Douglas to be patient, 'cause he was living proof that love makes things work. When MaBisha and Vernon got back, he put his love into action.

Vernon called everybody that had been at the wedding and told them to come on Friday to see their slide show. But he told Douglas and Bernita to come on Thursday. Bernita didn't know this.

Bernita sure was happy to see her friend MaBisha. You would have thought they had been gone a year rather than a month. She had spent some time chatting with MaBisha and getting all excited on account of MaBisha was starting to show. Bernita told her that she had some real good ideas for the baby's nursery. Now, them ideas were the ones she had made for her own children, but she figured that a good idea is one that gets used.

"When's everybody else coming?" Bernita asked. It had finally hit Bernita that nobody else was there. Her timing was working real good. Right when she asked, Douglas rang the bell.

"Here's the company now," Vernon said.

Vernon had been working on a tray of little finger foods. When the bell rang, he was grinning from one ear over to the other. MaBisha looked like she wanted to say something, but Vernon gave her a look that said she better not.

When Vernon came back into the kitchen, he had that beautiful Douglas with him. Bernita was looking from Vern to MaBisha.

"Is somebody going to tell me what's going on?" Bernita asked. She was acting all mad, but everybody could tell better.

"I wanted to sneak and tell you, but my husband wanted it to be a surprise."

"Good to see you again, Bernita." Douglas was smiling his I-take-real-good-care-of-my-teeth smile. Ain't nothing nicer than a good smile on a good man.

"I'm going to come clean, Bernita," Vernon said. If this meeting didn't work, he wanted to make sure that Bernita didn't get too mad.

"Douglas begged me to help him see you again. I am such a happy man and I know what it's like to want somebody so much that it hurts."

Bernita smiled and gave in a little bit of herself.

"Alright already, how the hell are you?" she said, smiling at Douglas.

MaBisha and Vernon went into the den and left the kitchen to Bernita and Douglas. Doug took the chance and ran with it.

Douglas told Bernita about himself and he came to find out that they had more in common than they thought possible. Douglas told Bernita all about his childhood and how he had been raised by his aunt. He talked about being an artist; how it gave him peace and rescued his soul. That's when he talked about his past hurts and how it had always been hard for him to open his heart to love. He didn't know why, but for some reason, he felt a strong connection to Bernita. Me and Ray were listening and giggling like schoolkids. Douglas took his time saying the things he needed to say.

Bernita listened to Douglas and had to work hard at paying attention what he was saying. His voice was doing that thing to her so she had to try to stay focused. Bernita could see the cord that tied them together. They were both like the song says: motherless children, a long way from home.

Bernita told him about her life, but she left out a lot of the stuff about her exes. Douglas listened good. He liked the way Bernita said just enough to make you want to know the whole story. When she was done, he asked if he could hold her hand. Well, Bernita went and messed things up. That child had the nerve to ask him why. Well, everybody got they shortcomings. Here they had shared more with each other than they ever had with anybody else this quick. Douglas knew something about timing, all right. He knew that they were made for each other, but he could see that Bernita wasn't quite there.

"When you're ready to live and love, let me know," Douglas said.

He went into the den and told his friends good night. Then he told Vernon that he had a present for Bernita, and he would leave it out by the front door.

Vernon wanted to know what happened, but this time it was MaBisha who motioned for him to be quiet. She went to the kitchen and found Bernita still there. She was crying softly. She looked up at MaBisha and asked her, "Why can't I just be happy?"

MaBisha held her and rocked her, the same way Bernita had done for MaBisha a long time ago.

into the marvelous light

Somebody come and carry me into a seven-day kiss.

—SWEET HONEY IN THE ROCK

Bernita prayed and cried. She just couldn't shake the fear that had climbed back into the bed she made and was lying in. There were pieces of her life that were still missing, but she didn't know where to look to find them. Folks say when the student is ready the teacher appears. Well, there's always another side of anything. Even clear glass got two different sides. Clean just one side and you'll see what I'm saying.

The other part of the teacher appearin' when the student is ready is that the student has got to make sure they go to all they classes. Bernita had been ready for the first level, but she was scared to graduate to the next.

One day she was thinking over her life and all that had happened. Now, it's good to look back from time to time, but you really can't just stay there. Bernita finally realized how much not

having a father affected her. Up till then, she didn't see all that this
meant. As she prayed, meditated, and thought over her life, she got
a glimpse of the emptiness that was in the places where her father's
memories should have been. She thought of all the time and ways
a father would have made a difference for her. As she sat and
thought, her doorbell rang.

Back on the day when me and Goody went to that cemetery, he
told me something real important. You already knew that he had
a crush on me from the time we was young. Well, when he couldn't
get me, he figured that he would do the next best thing. If you
smart, you know right where I'm headed. Goody tried to get to
love Buster on account of we looked something alike. Buster wore
herself different from me, she was more mannish, but Goody saw
the sameness.

Goody didn't find out that Buster was pregnant till after he left
town for the Navy. Buster wouldn't see him no more and he was
real hurt. When your "it'll do" don't do, you gotta move on.

Somebody told somebody who told Goody that his old girlfriend had a baby and that she didn't like men no more. Everybody
figured that Goody leaving her had something to do with it. Folks
can sure be wrong about other people's lives.

Anyway, Goody stayed as far away from his past and his child
for as long as he could. He was good, but he wasn't perfect. He told
hisself the same thing a lot of young men do when they find themselves with a baby; that one time was not enough to get nobody
pregnant, and that it probably wasn't his. Years later, his heart told
him otherwise. You see when he was young, traveling all over the
world with the Navy, he wanted to stay far away from responsibil-

ity and everything else that came with it. A few years became a
bunch of years and as folks in the military will tell you, it really is
hard to get back home when you busy trying to make a home. As
he got older, Goody saw how his past was connected to his life and
his future.

Most runway fathers get that same pull when they get older.
Don't matter how much they ran around when they was young,
later on, most of them men will want to look their children in the
face to say I'm sorry. Some men don't ever get the chance. Years of
separation will harden them children's hearts, so they ain't open to
the father who left them when they needed him.

Goody's past was pulling at him when he came back and found
me. Well, you should know by now that Goody is Bernita's father.
He went and found Buster before he found me and she told him
that the child was his.

"Ain't no need to go looking for her though," Buster said. "She
don't even want to have nothing to do with me and I didn't run out
on her."

Goody didn't really leave Bernita, he left town. He just didn't
come back when he found out. Well, he didn't tell me none of this
right away. He was happy with how our love was going, and he
didn't know what that news might have done to me so he was taking his time. Understand this, don't ever get comfortable with
time; you always have less of it than you think.

After I died, Goody got stuck in the time where his heart was
broken. He sat in his pain for years. He started doing something
he hadn't done before; he went to drinking real heavy. Some folks
think that their relatives love drinking and drugging, but the truth
is they drink and drug to cover the shame and guilt that comes
from not doing what they should.

Well, I got to Goody through a song we used to dance to, "Lovely Day" by Bill Withers. We used to laugh at how it seemed like Bill ran out of words when he sang, "Lovely day, lovely day, lovely day, lovely day." Old Bill went on and on. One night, Goody was over at Tubby's drinking and that song came on and wouldn't quit. Goody started thinking 'bout our lives and love. He remembered my laugh and the way he made me smile. Then he went back on the day I died and how he had promised me that he would help me find my niece. It dawned on him that he had never told me that Bernita was his child, and that he was saving that for later. Well, truth hit him like lightening. He left his shot of Jack right there on the bar and got up from where he had been going for too long. The years had been moving but he'd been too still. Goody decided right then and there, that he was gonna give Bernita the lovely day I would have wanted him to.

He didn't waste no more time, he got the information he needed from Buster, who told him that he shouldn't call.

"I ain't gonna call," he said. "I'm gonna go and do what I should've a long time ago." He caught a plane, rented a car, and went right up to Bernita's apartment, like he'd been doing it all along.

Bernita answered the door to find Goody standing outside. She was looking at a slightly older, male version of herself. Before she could get a word out, Goody told her all that he was to her. He told her that he was her father and uncle all rolled into one. He said that if she would let him, he wanted to be a friend too.

"I guess I should've called first, but I didn't want you to hang up. Plus, I really needed to see you," Goody said.

Bernita let Goody in. After all, she had just found the person she didn't even know she had lost. Goody told her all about me, and how I had changed when I met him. Bernita was quiet about it at first, then she told him that she had seen me for herself. Now it was Goody who didn't say nothing. After a good while he laughed and said, "That sure do sound like my Babe." A part of him wished that I had come to him, but the rest of him knew that Bernita needed me more. Besides, when I caught up with Bernita, I connected with him too. He thought of Bernita as his and my daughter. I had to admit that was more true than not. Good, bad, or otherwise, I had left a mark on Bernita just like she was my own.

Goody stayed at a hotel that was close by. Him and Bernita went to lunch every day. She got around to bringing him by her work. At first MaBisha thought that Goody was the reason that Bernita didn't take to old Douglas. When she found out that Goody was her father, she got all happy and cried. Her body was getting bigger and bigger. That baby was helping her to feel things deeper than she ever had. She cried at just about anything that was beautiful. When folks get brought together, it's one of the most beautiful things on earth.

God sure do know how to soften a person up. If Goody had shown up before he did, Bernita would not have been ready. She would have put him through the same hard time that most children do to a runaway parent who tries to come back home. Bernita didn't do none of the where you been? and what-took-you-so-long-mess. She fell right into step with the love that she was learning to receive.

Now when I tell you that all things work together for the good, you better just go ahead and rejoice.

One day Goody came to take Bernita to lunch and he saw a big package wrapped in brown paper. Bernita had not taken the painting Douglas left for her, so Vernon brought it over to the shelter, but she wouldn't even open it. She thought if she saw Douglas's art, she would feel too much of him. When her father came to work, he did what she couldn't.

"Ooo wee. What you got over here?" Goody said. (You already know that my man's country.)

Before Bernita could speak, Goody had opened that paper. The colors on that picture were real bright. It looked like they were daring you to turn away. If you took up that dare, you would lose sure enough. I told you that I didn't know much about art when I was alive. Now that I'm dead, I see artists as messengers of divine beauty and truth. This picture was bright and loud. There were pieces of things that looked like they didn't fit, but if you stared at it long though, you could see a man and a woman holding each other.

"That's real nice," Goody said. It looks like a Douglas Ford."

Don't ever get to thinking that country folks don't know nothing, just 'cause they live in the country. Goody had been all over the world, but he was still from down the way. In his travels, he learned a lot about art and other stuff. He said Douglas was one of his favorite artists.

When Bernita told him the story behind the painting, he looked at her and said, "It sure is better to be late than to never show up. If you ever needed me, you sure do need me now."

answering the call

Touch me in the morning.
—DIANA ROSS

Goody did what I couldn't do directly. He talked our child into going to see Douglas. Then he drove her there, but he let her go inside by herself.

"It'll be all right," he told her. He sounded like he had been giving her advice from the day she was born.

Douglas lived and worked in one of them big loft things. It was real modern, but he had a lot of real nice antiques. He collected furniture that had been made by the people who had been slaves.

Bernita rang his buzzer five times before he answered.

"Go away, I'm working."

Before he could go away from the wall where the buzzer was, Bernita yelled, "No, wait, it's me."

Normally when Douglas worked, he didn't talk to nobody. But

Bernita wasn't a nobody. For him she was everybody. Still, he didn't want her to do another number on his heart.

"Come up," he said.

Inside, he was dancing, but Bernita's fear had been contagious, so he tried not to let his real joy show.

When Bernita got up to Douglas' home, she saw more of the wonderful art. The walls seemed to be moving with the life of his work.

"You here to make me even crazier?" Douglas asked. He was trying hard not to smile.

I really did like the way this boy was working. Sometimes you gotta give back a little bit of what you been getting.

"As a matter of fact, I am."

Bernita went right straight from the heart. She told Douglas that she finally found her father and the piece of herself that kept her from being afraid. Then she did the first thing that came up in her head. She walked right up to Douglas Ford and told him she was ready to face her fears. That's when he told her she ain't have nothing to be afraid of. He grabbed her and they held on to each other till one of them got to kissing. You couldn't tell who started it, because it seemed like they both went for each other at the same time. When they were done, Bernita asked him why he had been so bold when they first met.

"It made me scared," she told him.

"It's never been my style to be bold like that. It just felt like love was calling me. And you know what the song says."

Bernita did. She didn't just recite the lyrics, she went on and sang those words with style. "When love calls, you better answer . . ."

"Sing it to me, baby," Douglas said and embraced her again.

one more thing

Life and love keep on coming. You open yourself up to goodness and it opens itself to you. MaBisha and Vernon had the biggest baby boy I ever saw. He looked like he could go to work with his father right then.

He made everybody smile. If you looked at him real close, you could see some of the ancestors looking right back at you. It seemed like he knew more than the folks who was holding him.

Bernita took down those walls that had formed around her heart and her soul. She and Douglas got married like they sometimes do in Africa. They just did it. They didn't have a lot of family to invite, but they had the friends they needed. Goody went down to Sylvania and brought Buster back to see her child. Buster and Bernita got on real good. Douglas found out that Buster had a real talent for art too. He teaches her something new every time they see each other.

If a child don't get to do what they was made for, they will run off into some of everything else. Buster didn't get to find her talent to create until she got older. Up until then, that talent got turned around. She was born to lift up people, not beat them up.

Life kept on getting better, but what happened next just ran on off with the cake. Buster and Goody didn't ever love each other with their bodies, but that didn't stop their love. They live and love together now in they own way. Life is sure strange.

I told you that I would let you know what happened to Van. Well, I ain't lied yet, have I?

Van and Tricia got real paranoid about each other. Van thought that Tricia was trying to poison him, and she was waiting for the fatal blow from him. She was sneaking from one corner of that apartment to the next, and he was starving himself.

They could have gone on like that a little longer, till one day the landlord came by to see if they had anything to put toward the rent.

"I'll let you go for now, but you gotta come up with something," he told them. "Too bad you can't paint. Did you hear about the artist who sold a painting for a million dollars and then turned around and gave the money to his wife? She turned around and used it to help build a place for families in trouble."

The landlord held up the paper for Van and Tricia to see. They looked at the paper and then at each other.

Bernita and Douglas sure did look good together. Didn't I tell you, that the best revenge is your happiness?

I don't know what happened after that to Van and Tricia. When Bernita let them go and got her joy, they didn't have no power over her, so I didn't have no interest in them. I don't know what happened to them, and I don't even much care.

Now I saved this part for last. Remember that letter that Vernon got in the package from his aunt? Well, I told you I would come back to it, and late is way better than never. Turns out that even though ole Ray was a real ladies' man, he fell hard for Douglas's mother. She was the one who sent him packing. Douglas's mother, Zelda, was what you would call a free spirit. She lived a very full but short life. Zelda made her transition right after Douglas was born. You ever notice that people who die young are some of the most wonderful folks who ever lived. When they make their transition, people say things like, "Why them, they were so good, they never said a mean thing to anybody?" Well, I'm gonna tell you what I know from being on the other side; them folks were born with the knowledge that they didn't have time to waste. That's why the good die young.

When Zelda met Ray, she loved him real fast. A week after they met, she was pregnant. She didn't tell Ray though. She just went on loving him, but when she started to show, she left town and went to live with her sister, the same one who raised Douglas. All she told Ray was that she loved him, but needed to move on.

Men just ain't used to talk like that from a woman. That hurt Ray something fierce. When he met Zelda, he finally decided to settle down. He was going to put an end to his cheating ways. Well, Zelda left, Douglas was born, and you know his story. But when Douglas read his father's letter, he found out just how little he knew about himself.

Dear Zelda,

I need you to know that I loved you more than anyone I ever been near. You was my breath, but you took it away. I've moved on with my life, but I can't get you out of my head. It's a hard thing too, 'cause now that I've tried to slow down, and not do all the cheating I used to, I feel like I'm being unfaithful. But this time, I'm cheating with a memory.

I've married a beautiful woman named Mavis, we have a big old happy boy named Vernon. I wish you could see him. He sure is my joy.

I don't know why I'm writing to you. I guess I'm just trying to let you go. Anyway, I hope you find the happiness you been looking for.

With love,
Ray Wilson

Ray never did get a chance to mail that letter. He was killed in a car crash the next day. Ray's sister took his stack of letters when she was helping his wife Mavis clear out Ray's things. She didn't want Mavis to be hurt by Ray's past.

Years later, when Ray's sister tried to find Zelda Ford, she learned that she had passed on, but that she'd had a boy by Ray. Now I know that I have been telling you a lot in a little space of time, but life unfolds that way. You can be going along at a normal pace and then *pow*, everything hits all at once.

Well, the day he got that package, Douglas called that aunt of his and asked all kinds of questions. She had already told him that his father was dead, but he wanted to find out about Ray's wife and son, his brother.

"His wife died, but her son lives in the same town as you," she told him.

She didn't have to say anything else. Douglas figured what you should be guessing too; Douglas and Vernon were not just brothers in spirit, they were brothers in blood.

When Douglas broke the news to Vernon, they both cried and hugged and cried some more. Then they were dancing and laughing like they had just found gold. When MaBisha and Bernita found out, they whooped and hollered like there was oil on that land too.

Now, I got time to tell you one more thing, so listen to me good. Life's journey can be real rough sometimes, but there's always help along the way. The next time you meet somebody and they seem real familiar, but you don't know why, just remember that love always finds its way home and when it comes calling, you better answer.

ACKNOWLEDGMENTS

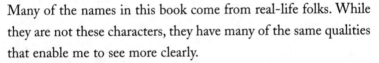

Many of the names in this book come from real-life folks. While they are not these characters, they have many of the same qualities that enable me to see more clearly.

Auta B. Wright is a real woman I met at a book signing. She said that her father wanted a boy. I loved the idea and asked her if I could alter her name and use it in the book. That's how I got Aunt Babe's name "Shoulda Been Wright." Ms. Auta B. is a beautiful elder, who allowed me to see that unique names are not unique to this generation. She also told me that *Redemption Song* reflected the stories of her ancestors. I am grateful to this beautiful woman who I met just once and was changed.

Bernita Brown is named after my sister and friend Bernita Berry, who is the chair of Social Work at Savannah State. Like Bernita Brown, she is hardworking, good, and caring. I am grateful to the many years of friendship and the resilience that her life represents.

Lee Morris is named for the high school music teacher Leander Morris. He is an ancestor now. In his life, he taught me to be strong, proud, on time, and worthy.

Lee Morris, in the book, represents a combination of those exceptional educators who do much more than teach: Harold Thompson, Karen Denton, Atlanta Brown, Mr. Jerome Pinkett (great counselor and mentor), Richard Wright, Karen Griffin, and many others.

I would also like to thank my editor and friend, Janet Hill, who has prayed me through the hardest year of my little life. My agent, Victoria Sanders, who laughs at my wacky ideas and then helps to make them possible.

The folks at Random House, who make me better than I am. Thank you for being dedicated to more than just the project.

BERTICE BERRY, Ph.D., is a lecturer, sociologist, and former stand-up comedian. She is also the author of four works of nonfiction and three previous novels, including *Redemption Song*, *The Haunting of Hip Hop*, and, most recently, *Jim and Louella's Homemade Heart-fix Remedy*. She lives in Savannah, Georgia, with her adopted children, eighty-six-year-old mother, and a host of ancestors who also keep her on the straight and narrow.